I0823904

Also by Julian Barnes

FICTION

Metroland
Before She Met Me
Flaubert's Parrot
Staring at the Sun
A History of the World in 10½ Chapters
Talking It Over
The Porcupine
Cross Channel
England, England
Love, etc.
The Lemon Table
Arthur & George
Pulse
The Sense of an Ending
The Noise of Time
The Only Story
Elizabeth Finch

NON-FICTION

Letters from London, 1990–1995
Something to Declare
The Pedant in the Kitchen
Nothing to Be Frightened Of
Through the Window
Levels of Life
Keeping an Eye Open
The Man in the Red Coat
Changing My Mind

TRANSLATION

In the Land of Pain
by Alphonse Daudet

DEPARTURE(S)

DEPARTURE(S)

JULIAN BARNES

Alfred A. Knopf
New York
2026

A BORZOI BOOK
FIRST HARDCOVER EDITION PUBLISHED BY ALFRED A. KNOPF 2026

Published by Alfred A. Knopf, a division of Penguin Random House LLC,
1745 Broadway, New York, NY 10019.

Knopf, Borzoi Books, and the colophon are registered trademarks of
Penguin Random House LLC.

Cataloging-in-Publication Data has been applied for with the Library of Congress.

ISBN: 978-0-593-80450-6 (hardcover)
ISBN: 978-0-593-80451-3 (eBook)

penguinrandomhouse.com | aaknopf.com

Printed in the United States of America
3rd Printing

The authorized representative in the EU for product safety and compliance is Penguin Random House Ireland, Morrison Chambers, 32 Nassau Street, Dublin D02 YH68, Ireland, https://eu-contact.penguin.ie.

Racheleli

DEPARTURE(S)

I
THE GREAT I AM

The other day, I discovered an alarming possibility. No, worse: an alarming fact.

I have an old friend, a consultant radiologist, who for years has been sending me clipppings from the *British Medical Journal*. She knows that my interest tends towards the ghoulish and the extreme. In my memory – that place where degradation and embellishment overlap – I have filed away cases of patients who exploded when a heated scalpel ignited their bodily gases, and others from the early days of the MRI scanner when internal metal stitches were shot like shrapnel into soft flesh. These stories are sometimes accompanied by photos: for instance, of a man who grew his toenails to such a curling length – several metres, as I recall – that for years he had been unable to walk. Then there is the medical profession's everyday task of removing unexpected objects which have been swallowed – like bags of nails – or forcibly indulged up the rectum. (In the old days, popular anal self-implants were miniature busts of Napoleon, a habit which doubtless added patriotism to pleasure.) And a case I particularly remember, of a man who had been fitted with a tracheostomy tube. When he went for a check-up, doctors were baffled by yellowish stains around the hole into which the tube was fixed. It turned out that the patient was a desperate smoker who, unable to inhale through his mouth any more, discovered that if he took out his tube, the cigarette fitted perfectly in the hole; all he had to do was light up and inflate his lungs. Men (and most of these bizarre activities were undertaken by men) can be most ingenious, even – or especially – when it goes against their own best interests.

The most recent clipping sent by Dr Jacky had, appropriately enough, a literary heading: 'Proust and madeleine: Together in the thalamus'. Naturally, I read on. 'Madeleine, you will recollect, was not the love of Proust's life but a biscuit that, when dropped into tea, created an involuntary autobiographical memory (IAM).' The report's source was the journal *Neurology Clinical Practice*, and its subject a forty-five-year-old man who had suffered a left posterothalamic haemorrhagic stroke. The consequences were much more extreme and particular than the gentle jolt Proust (and his fictional narrator) received from a madeleine – which is not exactly a 'biscuit', rather a plump little cake moulded in the fluted shape of a pilgrim's scallop. The patient disclosed that 'tasting apple pie would trigger memories of all the pies he had ever tasted; they would be experienced in proper chronology and would rush into his mind like a cascade'.

As I said, my first reaction was one of alarm: imagine such high-speed assaults by forgotten memories, a historic avalanche roaring across your perception of the present, tearing up your very sense of yourself. And, as a friend pointed out, what if the triggering experience was not as life-affirming as eating an apple pie? What, he said, if you farted, however quietly, and were then presented, in chronological order, with every single fart you had ever let loose? And so on – you can provide your own examples without difficulty. Imagine the exhausting thought – or sight – of a few thousand bacon sandwiches flashing through your consciousness (and would their quality and difference, plus your reactions to them, be replayed as well?).

I am now in my mid-seventies, and like most older people

am sometimes bored by myself – by which I mean my repetitious remembering of thoughts and deeds and, especially, opinions. (And those who never bore themselves, who continue to be publicly entertained by their own lives and their repeated anecdotes, are usually the worst bores on the planet. Men again, on the whole.) But the frenetic, assaulting boredom of high-speed IAMs is, for the moment anyway, unimaginable. Wouldn't it make you want to kill yourself?

My second reaction was more considered, and more writerly. IAMs would certainly help with autobiography. You think you have remembered something 'just so', and the more times you have remembered it and retold it, the more times you become convinced of its truth. But what if you were pulled up and corrected by . . . your own brain? What if it could lay in front of you all your retellings and demonstrate how gradually yet systematically you had diverged from your original account? Wouldn't that be weird and disorienting? Yet also helpful: you could hardly overrule your own thalamus, could you?

And what if your brain didn't just contain a chronological listing of all the pies you had eaten, but also of your moral actions and inactions? Every time you said 'I love you' whether you meant it or not. Every time you failed to say 'I love you' when you should have done, when you wanted to but failed. How would you face the record – the chronological record – of all your lies, hypocrisies, cruelties both avoidable and (seemingly) unavoidable, your harsh forgettings, your dissimulations, your broken promises, your infidelities of word and deed? Not just the actual failings but the imagined and desired ones. Remember President Jimmy Carter's celebrated interview about Lust in *Playboy* magazine, in which he boldly confessed that 'I've committed adultery in my heart many times.' We've most of us done that, while tending to retain in our conscious memories only the more charming and less guilt-inducing of our fantasies. But what about those more embarrassing, inadmissable, sluttish adulteries of the heart which we have chosen to suppress?

There was a second part to President Carter's famous admission which strikes me as even bolder. After confessing his dream-sins, he went on: 'This is something God recognises I will do – and I have done it – and God forgives me for it.' This seems, to a non-believer, more than a little smug. Not only will the Almighty forgive Jimmy Carter at the Final Judgement, but He is forgiving him *as he goes along*, each time his adulterous heart throbs. But perhaps presidents have a greater insight than the rest of us into the nature and magnanimity of the Godhead.

So here's another question that occurs: what if there were a way of producing IAMs without the patient – you, me – having to suffer a catastrophic stroke in the first place? Humans, after all, have been trepanning one another since Neolithic times – boring holes in the skull to let demons and evil spirits and madness out, to relieve pressure on the brain, to alleviate epilepsy and other mental disorders. In early sixteenth-century northern European painting, there was a popular sub-theme entitled 'The Extraction of the Stone of Madness'. In its best-known example, by Hieronymus Bosch, a plump elderly peasant leans back on a wooden throne while a surgeon, wearing a tin funnel on his head, chops into his patient's forehead. (Though the funnel apparently indicates that the surgeon is a charlatan.)

What if a precise hole could be bored in the skull and an

infinitesimal amount of damage done with the aim of provoking the full release of our memories? It's hard, admittedly, to imagine a neurosurgeon agreeing to such a procedure or being convinced of its social benefit ('I want to remember my mother better' or 'It would be a great help writing my autobiography' are reasons unlikely to convince). There is also a long, if usually undistinguished, history of self-trepanning, so perhaps some brave soul suffering a bout of amnesia or early-onset dementia might persuade himself – and again, the foolhardy candidate is likely to be a man – of the procedure's feasibility. A dentist's drill seems to be one popular way of self-trepanning. Crackpots do it to 'promote brain blood flow'; also to create – almost literally – that 'third eye' which supposedly leads to spiritual enlightenment.

But imagine further that it became at some point both surgically feasible and also lawful: might you fancy it? Perhaps initially, volunteers could be bribed to undergo the procedure, supposing it to be no worse than selling their blood.

IAM is just a necessary, inevitable acronym. Yet separate the first and second letters and you get I AM. Which is pertinent. Memory is identity, as we often repeat to ourselves. If so, all the IAMs stored inside us will add up to who and what we are and have been. And beyond this lies the phrase The Great I AM, a way of referring to the Christian God. Who used to punish or reward us because He remembered every single action we had performed, and every thought and emotion which had run through us. Though many still believe that a Last Judgement awaits them after death, there is now a rival, pre-death judgement potentially available, one that has been updated and secularised. Our catalogue of sins is not inscribed in St Peter's monumental book of record, but lies within our own brain. All it would take, perhaps, is a team of neurologists to find the key.

Though who, then, would be playing God? Not the head surgeon, who would merely be a skilled facilitator. So we would be the ones left as judges. Which might lead to self-indulgence. Unless, on the contrary, it forced us to grow up.

I found out more about the case of the man who remembered every pie he'd ever eaten. His IAMs began occurring nine months after his stroke, and their timeline covered his entire life, from his very first year (which we are supposed not to be able to remember) up until the present day. The trigger could be touch, smell, taste or sight. On one occasion, the scent of fresh dough set off a memory from childhood – that of walking barefoot in his grandmother's kitchen while holding his mother's hand. He saw again his grandmother's apron and experienced 'the round feeling of the soles of my feet'. All of which sounds very Proustian.

But a 'cascade' of memories would sometimes arrive without any specific sensory cue: one day, he remembered in full detail a family visit to the 1967 Montreal Expo, made when he was three. Further, and strangely perhaps, it turned out that his day-to-day memory improved following his stroke. He also discovered that he could voluntarily suppress his bouts of IAMs if he chose to. Such an off-switch would presumably be a great relief to the endurer; and if you were, say, writing your autobiography, then you might be able to pause and edit the tirade of information belching from your brain as you went along. And maybe in time an on-switch might be found, and you could access the entire contents of your past, as and when you wished. A question: would you want to know absolutely everything about yourself? Is that a good idea, or a bad one?

Which leads to a further question. Is it correct to refer to that visual cascade of all the pies you've ever eaten as 'memories'? Because what we conventionally think of as a memory is something which has been remembered, frequently or infrequently, over the course of our lives, mutating a little with each retelling until it congeals finally into a version which we convince ourselves is the truth. But when the original subject of that clinical report experienced a 'full detailed passage' of going to the Montreal Expo, this would, presumably, be something he had not previously remembered (though his family had doubtless told him about it). So it would not be a normally degraded memory but rather a re-presentation of the original experience, a correct revival not of what the grown man remembered, but of what the boy's brain received on that forgotten day all those years ago. More than even a 'virginal memory', it would be *the event itself*, as processed by the brain back then. Might that perhaps tempt you to a spot of self-trepanning?

Two things to mention at this stage:

1) There will be a story – or a story within the story – but not just yet; and
2) This will be my last book.

I theorised that the constant, furious assault of unwanted – or at least unasked-for – high-speed IAMs might make you want to kill yourself. Perhaps that's an exaggeration. But unless, like Pie-man, you can find some way of switching it off, it would certainly interfere with your normal life. In his classic study

The Mind of a Mnemonist the Soviet neuropsychologist A. R. Luria described the case of 'S', who first came into Luria's life in the 1920s. S had a formidable memory, whose functioning and techniques were examined in laboratory conditions over a period of thirty years. He was able to remember sequences of letters and numbers, phrases and stray words, with extraordinary accuracy, and could recall such tests in perfect detail more than a decade later. One method he used was ascribing eidetic images to key words:

> Say I'm given the word *elephant*: I'd see a zoo. If they gave me *America*, I'd set up an image of Uncle Sam; if *Bismarck*, I'd place my image near the statue of Bismarck; and if I had the word *transcendent*, I'd see my teacher Sherbiny standing and looking at a monument.

S was also afflicted by synaesthesia, which added to his daily load. Every sound he heard would be accompanied by light and colour. Asked if he remembered a particular fence, he replied that of course he did: 'It has such a salty taste and feels so rough; furthermore, it has such a sharp, piercing sound.' When he goes to a restaurant, 'I decide what I'm going to eat according to the name of the food, the sound of the word. It's silly to say that mayonnaise tastes good. The z [as in the Russian spelling] ruins the taste – it's not an appealing sound . . . And if a menu is badly written, I simply can't eat – the menu seems so filthy.' It all sounds exhausting, and it was; any sudden noise or distraction when S tried to access a memory would cause 'puffs of steam' or 'splashes' which obliterated what he was trying to read. And since, inevitably, S became a music-hall turn, benign or malign attempts from the audience to help or hinder produced an incredible strain.

And what of the effect of all this on his personality and private life? Luria's initial impression of S was of 'a rather ponderous and timid person', but one whose 'memories of early childhood were incomparably richer than ours'. In his adult life, he changed jobs dozens of times before becoming a professional mnemonist, when his problem-solving and feats of memory gave him a living. But away from that, his strange gift often disabled him. For instance, he was virtually unable to read a book, because people he remembered from other books with similar characteristics kept forcing themselves into the text before him. It was almost impossible for him to read poetry, as figurative thinking and language baffled him. As he told Luria several times, 'I can only understand what I can visualise.' And he couldn't *not* remember; he couldn't disengage that part of his brain. To others, he had all the appearance of a dreamer; time passed without him noticing. His conversation involved endless digressions: he was constitutionally unable to stick to the same subject. So if you mentioned the word 'horse' to him, 'There's also its colour and taste I have to consider.'

This distractability gave him an air of helplessness, which led people to take him for 'a dull, awkward, somewhat absent-minded fellow'. Luria noted that S had a family – 'a fine wife and a son who was a success' – but this too he perceived as through a haze. 'Indeed,' Luria concluded, 'one would be hard put to say which was more real for him: the world of the imagination in which he lived, or the world of reality in which he was a temporary guest.' This seems a terrifyingly unenviable condition: to be a temporary guest in one's own life.

The famous incident of the madeleine dipped in tea and savoured by Proust's narrator Marcel isn't, as set down in the text, an involuntary autobiographical memory or IAM; rather, it is a very leisurely, semi-voluntary, semi-automatic memory or VLSVSAM, hardly a memorable acronym. At various points in the novel Marcel is aware of some kind of essential, deeper reality which is out – or down – there, largely inaccessible to us but waiting to be captured, or recaptured. The first of these near-transcendent moments occurs early in the novel. Marcel is reflecting on Combray, the small country town where he spent childhood holidays with his grandparents, and where his daily walks followed one of two directions – *du côté de chez Swann* or *du côté de chez Guermantes* – walks which symbolically prefigure the two social classes his later life will be split between: the rich, cultured bourgeoisie, and an aristocracy which scorned the middle classes but would ultimately be consumed by them.

Marcel finds that when he tries to remember Combray, only the frustrating norms of memory apply: he sees it as no more than 'a luminous panel, sharply defined against a vague and shadowy background'. And he sees the same scenes again and again. This, he realises, is because they are prompted by 'voluntary memory, the memory of the intellect', and since 'the pictures which that kind of memory shows us preserve nothing of the past itself', he no longer has any interest in trying to 'ponder over this residue of Combray. To me it was in reality all dead.'

But then a wonderful thing happens. One day, many years later, low in spirits, he returns home, and his adored mother, seeing that he is cold, offers him some tea, 'a thing I did not ordinarily take'. Further, she sends out for a *petite madeleine*. He dips a morsel of cake into the tea and raises it to his lips in a spoon; as he tastes it, an exquisite pleasure runs through him. It is beyond gustatory; it is soul-changing.

His daily mood – 'mediocre, contingent, mortal' – vanishes, and he accesses, with an 'all-powerful joy', some essence of himself.

And Combray? Not so fast. He takes a second mouthful, in which he finds nothing more than with the first; then a third, in which he finds less. 'It is time to stop: the potion is losing its magic.' He considers this for a while, then makes a final attempt to force himself back into that joyful moment when he had taken his first morsel of tea-soaked cake. Whereupon something rises up inside of him, dragged from the depths of his self, 'mounting slowly' with 'the echo of great spaces traversed'. Something seems about to appear, then slips back into the abyss. He tries *ten times* to pull whatever it is from wherever it was.

'And suddenly the memory revealed itself.' This is not 'the voluntary memory, the memory of the intellect', but something deeper and more distant. It is not the sight of the madeleine that has triggered it – he has seen thousands of such cakes in the intervening years – but something more primitive and essential: 'taste and smell alone, more fragile but more enduring'. And so he finds himself back once again in Combray, visiting his Aunt Léonie on a Sunday morning, when she would dip a little piece of madeleine in her lime tea and feed it to him. Memories now unfold before him just as, in the traditional Japanese pastime, torn pieces of paper placed in water unfold into flowers. Combray and all its forgotten parts are restored to him in their original colours and forms. He remembers how 'the good folk of the village and its surroundings, taking shape and solidity, sprang into being, towns and gardens alike, from my cup of tea'.

A few notes on this. First, Proust distinguishes 'voluntary memory, the memory of the intellect' from involuntary memory, which allows access to something deeper and more essential. Yet as he describes it, the process most definitely involves the will – Marcel tries ten times to drag those deep-sunk memories out of himself. It may be involuntary to begin with (the unexpected tea/madeleine combination) but it seems to involve a large measure of the voluntary – choosing to follow that smell and taste, straining on the hawser of memory. Secondly, when he succeeds in recovering his fullest memories of Combray, it turns out that, as described, they don't seem qualitatively different from those achieved by the banal and limited voluntary memory: 'the good folk of the village and their little dwellings', and so on. What Marcel tells us he now sees, or re-sees, is more comprehensive than what his voluntary memory has previously revealed. But is there more 'essence' and 'reality' to it? Not to this reader.

Perhaps my scepticism comes from the fact that I've never had such a transcendental memory; I've subsisted on the hard rusks of voluntary memory. I asked a few close friends, and they hadn't had a Proustian unfolding either. I suspect that nowadays those keen to access what has been long forgotten might try either psychotherapy or some mind-altering drug like LSD to open the doors of memory and perception. Would I do that myself? Probably not. But then I have never found myself, as Marcel was, frustrated by the limits of the intellect's memory; and I doubt that if I could reaccess Acton W3 in the late 1940s and early 50s, all would open like a Japanese flower in water, reminding me of forgotten things and forgotten happiness. Nor can I guess what sudden olfactory key might work on me: certainly not a fortuitous morsel of soggy cake. More likely the smell of the glue and varnish I used when constructing model aircraft, or the aroma of frying bacon, or that of a damp golden retriever.

*

In her essay 'Sketch of the Past', Virginia Woolf (who both admired Proust and envied him) linked Combray to the possible future world of IAMs with a strange brilliance:

> I suppose, that my memory supplies what I have forgotten, so that it seems as if it were happening independently, though I am really making it happen. In certain favourable moods, memories – what one has forgotten – come to the top. Now if this is so, is it not possible – I often wonder – that things we have felt with great intensity have an existence independent of our minds; are in fact still in existence? And if so, will it not be possible, in time, that some device will be invented by which we can tap them? I see it – the past – as an avenue lying behind; a long ribbon of scenes, emotions. There at the end of the avenue still, are the garden and the nursery. Instead of remembering here a scene and there a sound, I shall fit a plug into the wall; and listen to the past. I shall turn up August 1890. I feel that strong emotion must leave its trace; and it is only a question of discovering how we can get ourselves again attached to it, so that we shall be able to live our lives through from the start.

As well as the IAM, there is another phenomenon known as the HSAM, or 'highly superior autobiographical memory'. There are only a hundred or so known cases who enjoy, or suffer from, this capability. One such is an eighteen-year-old Canadian woman who can describe not only what she did on any single day in her life, but the clothes she was wearing and what she ate. Each day, she says, is filed away in her brain like a 'little movie' which she can replay at will. It's hard to imagine any upside to such a superabundance of granular self-knowledge; but easy to see a major downside – that of being unable to edit, diminish or discard unwanted memories. Let alone painful ones: whereas for the rest of us time may dull their sharpness, and even allow us to forget, for her they will always remain as unpleasantly vivid as when they were first experienced. And beyond this, what could be the possible use of having all one's past continually available, except to fund some theatrical or TV act, as with Luria's mnemonist?

We talk of 'the tricks that memory plays on us' – yet who would envy someone with HSAM? No tricks at all, just constant, unavoidable, trick-free memory . . . You would surely begin to envy those with a 'normal' memory – i.e., spotty, unreliable, and even mischievous. One of the brain's more spiteful ploys is so-called cryptomnesia, in which the subject is presented with a forgotten memory but fails to recognise it as such, imagining it instead to be something new and original. This phenomenon was first identified in 1874 by an English spiritualist medium with the crypto-spiritualist name of Stainton Moses. Unsurprisingly, it is often associated with plagiarism and fraud. But the most famous, and seemingly genuine, case of cryptomnesia concerns Nietzsche, who at one point in the text of *Thus Spake Zarathustra* repeated word for word an incident from a book published half a century previously. Plagiarism? Not so, according to Nietzsche's sister: she confirmed that her brother had indeed read the original text when he was between twelve and fifteen, at which point his memory was already formidable. Yet by the time he wrote *Zarathustra* he was suffering from considerable cognitive degeneration, combined with monomania. His sister was convinced that this 'resurfacing memory' had truly struck Nietzsche as an original thought he himself had just generated. Forgetting your own memories – or rather, appropriating the words of others and thinking them brand-new ideas – it's a rich field. At times, it seems as if the brain is just toying with us.

The existence of IAMs, and our acknowledgement of them, will also, I realise, change our relationship with our own brains. It's hard to think about the brain, because it involves using that very same brain to do so: a complicated and perhaps in the end futile enterprise. Yet most of us feel that we are somehow in charge of our brains, rather – though this might be the wrong metaphor – as a submarine captain is in charge of his vessel. Periscope up! Scan the horizon! Intruders ahoy! And so on. We imagine that we tell our brains in which direction to point its torpedoes, and when to fire them. Yet such an assumption of orderliness and control on our part doesn't really stand up to scrutiny. Our brains have far more on us than we have on them: they know all that we know, whereas we know only some of what they do.

We are told that the average brain processes seventy-four gigabytes of information every day. Or, to put it differently, 70,000 thoughts. It whirrs away, day and night. We sleep but the brain doesn't. It may lower its activity during the night, but it never shuts down until we finally shut down. (No, reverse that priority: we shut down finally when it shuts down.) So another way of thinking about the brain is to consider it as the monarch of super-computers. We need to know stuff, and the brain tells us what is what, faster than Google.

But this again may be the wrong model. It still gives us too much agency. It still makes us imagine that we are in charge of our brains, and of what we want from them. But we are much more passive than that. As a philosopher friend pointed out to me, the brain can't let us know everything it is processing as it goes along: that would overwhelm us, flood us with far too much information, reduce us to some quivering, whimpering animal. The brain, she went on, only informs us on a need-to-know basis. This is much closer to reality, and suggests yet another metaphor, another of my temporary certainties. Think of espionage, the world of John le Carré. Think of the brain as the Circus, the novelist's name for the headquarters of British intelligence. Think of ourself – our self – as an agent running in the field, being told only part of a much wider picture, just enough for us to behave plausibly and fulfil our functions. Though as we know, agents in the field can be cut loose, disowned, starved of funds and information, betrayed. 'Control' is running us. But at the same time we 'are' our brains. Even le Carré can't compete with all the complications and subterfuges of this.

I wrote the two preceding paragraphs (in first draft) at 4.50 on a Thursday morning, with my electric typewriter, near to an open window, making the only noise in a darkened street. I did so because I had been lying awake, my brain quietly idling, when it suddenly nudged me with the phrase 'need to know', which my philosopher friend had used at about eight o'clock on the Tuesday evening. (So does that make it an involuntary memory or a semi-voluntary one?) But I couldn't be sure – having had much previous evidence to the contrary – that my brain would remind me of it again in the morning. So I got out of bed and wrote the phrase, and then the thoughts above which led to and from it. However vivid an idea is in the middle of the night, you can't expect your brain to remember it – and remind you of it – a few hours later. It's not, after all, your factotum.

A final, pedantic, thought. How could the Pie-man (or his medical observers) be sure that his cascade of memory contained *all* the pies he had ever eaten? Some might have been forgotten, others perhaps imagined; nor would it be possible to prove that they arrived in exact (or even approximately exact) chronological order. Perhaps some editing process or synaptic weakening had taken place of which he was unaware, and he was being re-shown only a percentage of crusts and their contents? But even so . . .

Proust's famous Madeleine Incident comes at the end of the 'Overture' to the first volume of *À la Recherche*. It is immediately followed by 150 pages of 'Combray', where the town, its inhabitants and their doings are described in forensic – or Proustian – detail. But we don't really imagine, do we, that all this authorial remembering has come from a cup of tea? Proust clearly believes in the powerful unloosing effect on our memory of taste and smell: in the second volume, *À l'Ombre des jeunes filles en fleurs*, he repeats that 'The best part of our memory lies outside ourselves, in a rainy breath, in the smell of a closed-up room or the smell of the first blaze of a fire.' But perhaps the Madeleine Incident, however true in life, should be regarded as a fictional device as much as a transcendental key. Perhaps Proust was a novelist in search of a theory to scaffold his work – which would be a very French thing.

We can and should trust novelists when they tell us the beautiful lies of their fiction. But we are allowed to be genially sceptical when they talk about their working methods (those heavy hours they all claim to put in) and disclose 'where they get their ideas from'. Proust, for instance, always maintained that he learned about involuntary memory from the philosopher Henri Bergson. Since Bergson was Proust's cousin by marriage, and wrote a great deal about memory, the matter seemed for a long time incontrovertible. However, it has now become less plausible, for two reasons. The first is that while Bergson distinguishes between rote-learning memory and 'spontaneous' memory (which reveals stored-up perceptions and impressions in sudden flashes), he never discusses involuntary memory in its full, Proustian sense. The second reason relates to a disastrous six weeks Proust spent in a clinic on the edge of the Bois de Boulogne.

Despite – or perhaps because of – being the son of a doctor, the novelist had a great disbelief in medicine. He described it as 'a compendium of successive and contradictory mistakes on the part of doctors'. For years he kept promising his mother that he would seek a cure for his lifelong asthma, but only did so after her death in 1905. The clinic he chose was run by Paul Sollier, one of the great neurologist Charcot's most brilliant pupils. His work was wide-ranging: he wrote on hysteria, alcoholism, epilepsy, hiccups, anorexia, tabes dorsalis, gambling, the mental states of the dying, and miracles. He also developed a system for comparing the mental condition of so-called 'normal' people, which eventually led to the creation of the IQ test. Proust had chosen Sollier over rival neurologists partly because the treatment he offered was shorter, and partly because of Sollier's interest in homosexuality. The course theoretically consisted of isolation therapy: patients would be confined to bed for the first week and given an entirely milk-based diet. This regime, known as '*au lit et au lait*', was common at the time: the diarist Jules Renard, diagnosed in 1909 with emphysema and arteriosclerosis, spent the last year of his life on it. In Proust's case the theory was that it would provoke psychological regression, making the patient more dependent on the physician and thus easier to treat.

But the six weeks got off to a bad start. During their first conversation, Proust asked Sollier if he had read Bergson. 'Yes, I felt I ought to,' came the reply, 'because we're both interested in the same field. But I find him terribly confused and narrow.' Proust told a friend: 'I felt a Da Vincian smile of intellectual pride passing over my face, and this didn't contribute to the success of my therapeutic treatment.' Nor did the writer's stubborn resistance to 'isolation therapy'. Sollier, perhaps recognising the intractability of his patient, allowed Proust to continue with his enormous daily correspondence, by either dictation or his own hand; and he was permitted visitors for two hours every Tuesday, Thursday and Saturday afternoons. Proust subsequently complained that his stay at the clinic was not just useless, but counterproductive, and that he had returned home 'fantastically ill'. This may or may not be true. Proust's biographer George Painter remarked that 'He behaved towards them [doctors], as to his father, with apparent submission and real evasion.'

Sollier's name was forgotten for a long time, his oblivion increased when his institute and all its records were destroyed by Allied bombing of the nearby Renault factory in March 1942. But Proust's six-week stay was far from 'counterproductive', as he claimed. Sollier was fascinated by the notion of involuntary memory. He wrote that our mechanism for the voluntary retrieval of the past is far less efficient than we imagine: 'Our will really plays a trivial part in the evocation of memories, and it is an illusion to believe that it is under the influence of free and voluntary efforts that this evocation takes place.' For instance: 'I am feeling a violent emotion during an accident which I have witnessed, and this emotional state triggers in me a revival of memories which bear no relation to the actual accident, but have determined in me a similar emotional state.' It seems inconceivable that Proust didn't get some of his ideas from Sollier, either in person or through the latter's books. And his only written mention of the clinician's name is a giveaway. In a 1908 notebook of Proust's, next to some jottings on involuntary memory, there it is: 'Sollier'.

2

THE BEGINNING OF THE STORY

The story comes in two parts, as it was lived in two parts, with a long gap between them. But also, because my account will have two different textures. For its first half, I am entirely reliant on memory, plus a photograph or two. (What did T. S. Eliot say about memory? That no matter how you wrap it in camphor, the moths will get in.) By the time of the second half, I was a writer, and had been one for many years. So I kept notebooks – usually simultaneous with events – and diaries, usually written up within a few days or weeks. You might assume that such documentation would be more trustworthy than the moth-eaten memories of long ago. But I am not sure of this (I am sure of fewer things nowadays). What I document is what I want to remember – so one sort of triage is taking place – and/or what I think might be useful in some future piece of writing – so another kind of triage. But it would be foolish to deduce that these detailed annotations of life amount to *what actually happened*. I often overlook or forget things of importance: the rush towards certainty can lead one astray.

What follows is a true story, though it comes with several caveats. First, I have changed the names of the two central characters, for the simple reason that I promised each of them, separately, that I would never write about them. (And yes, I follow you: if I broke that oath, how dependable is my promise to you of authenticity?) But people often tell me their stories, not because I am a writer; rather, despite the fact that I am a writer. I am interested in most human lives, and perhaps have – or used to have – a manner which invites others to confide. Sometimes they say beforehand, nervously, 'You won't use this, will you?' Or, less often, and more confidently, 'I've got a story for you.' And to both I reply, 'That's not how it works.' Which is true. Mostly I write fiction, which requires the slow composting of life before it becomes useable material, and I have no notion at the time what might or might not break down into fictional possibility. And the same applies, to a lesser extent, to non-fiction. As with the story of Stephen and Jean below.

My second caveat is one which other ageing writers might sympathise with. In order to tell the story – any story – I have to give a certain amount of background. You know the form: who, where, when, why; what the weather was like and if that is relevant; who the characters are and how they speak; their social roots and educational background, their career paths. Who was prematurely balding, who had her crow's feet surgically sandpapered, what their masturbatory habits were at different stages of their lives. Actually, just writing this makes me feel a bit weary. And I wouldn't blame you if you did too. So I'll keep most of that stuff to a minimum. You may thank me, or you may not. But as writers get older, either they grow egotistically expansive or they think: contain yourself and cut to the chase. Verdi once observed that in old age he 'learned how to write less music'. And no, I'm not comparing myself to Verdi.

My final caveat is, as I said, that this story has a large hole in the middle: a period of forty years or so when I saw neither of its chief participants. So I can only offer the beginning and the end of the story. Neither of them did more than sketch in for me the missing middle. And since none of us ever suffered a left posterothalamic haemorrhagic stroke, I am in this first part relying on our three overlapping memories, with all their daily casual faults, for my truth. A question: if we did have access via IAMs to what 'really happened' in our lives, would that make autobiography (and fiction-writing) easier or harder? I suspect they would become harder.

The three of us met at Oxford. At which words I pause. Many years ago, in my novel *Flaubert's Parrot*, the narrator gave a list (with which I largely agreed) of subjects which should be banned from fiction on a temporary or permanent basis. Proscription number 4 began: 'There is to be a twenty-year ban on novels set in Oxford or Cambridge, and a ten-year ban on other university fiction.' This ordinance, I calculate, actually ran out in 2004, when, without telling anyone, I renewed it for another twenty years. So, if this were a piece of fiction, I would be obliged to pack the three of us off to university in Bristol or Sussex or Manchester.

Anyway, I studied at Oxford between 1964 and 1968 (and you can google that if you wish). I was at Magdalen, one of the grander, older colleges – and, back then, all-male. It had its own deer park – we would be served venison on Founder's Day – some rare kind of fritillary growing in the water meadow, and a river running round, if not through, the grounds. There was punting, and a marginal yet strong awareness that we were following in privileged footsteps. I shan't elaborate: you'll have seen it in a hundred films and TV dramas, though usually without the scholarship and grammar-school boys, the acne, dandruff, and the terrifying lack of self-confidence – intellectual, social, moral. At times it felt as if we were inauthentically replicating a style of life that had originally been enacted – and still was, by others – with full self-belief.

(A memory. At school – googlable, City of London, 1957–64 – we had a maths master called Horace Brearley. Though I had given up maths at fifteen, he was somehow in charge of a special class during my last weeks there. Perhaps it was about 'civics', or a special one-off briefing for those going up to university. One afternoon, Mr Brearley said to us, 'And always remember that your time there will be the best years of your life.' This prophecy occasionally hung heavy over me while I was at Oxford. 'Is this as good as it will get?' I used to wonder, and would sink into gloom. Brearley had a son called Michael, who was the school's captain of cricket. He went on to captain the England team, and then became a psychoanalyst. At school, he was four years older than me – well, he still is – and so I naturally never encountered him. But I followed his career, and in 2022, both of us now grey-to-white-headed, we happened to meet at a dinner. He asked if I remembered his father. I said that I did, and repeated those words of his which had been half-prediction, half-instruction, and which I had resented for many years. Michael paused, seemingly puzzled. 'He never told *me* that,' he commented.)

I messed up my undergraduate career, for what it's worth; though 'career' makes it sound more purposeful than it was. I went up to read Modern Languages (French and Russian), but decided after two terms that they weren't 'serious' enough subjects – I could read the literature on my own, I thought – and switched to Philosophy and Psychology. But these in turn proved rather too 'serious' for the brain that I had at the time, and after another two terms I returned, with humiliated irritation, to the study of French. The college told me that they expected me to get a First; unsurprisingly, I got a Second.

All of which is relevant only because, thanks to my bifurcated 'career', I got to know Stephen and Jean separately, and, through me, they discovered each other. Earlier writers might have described me as 'the instrument of their fate' – the more so when, decades later, I fulfilled that role a second time. But

I'm not a believer in the high tone, and in any case the Tragic Age is long past: we are not grand enough to justify such words. We still use them, to be sure – 'What a Tragedy that was!' we exclaim when things go wrong, when cancer strikes, when a middling politician is disgraced, when an innocent child is killed in the normal, hazardous way of sublunary existence. Maybe we haven't yet found the right words to fit the lesser nature of the post-tragic life. Or maybe today's stories somehow encode the missing words. I'll leave this to you. All I'd say here is, I wasn't trying to 'play God' – not in the least.

Back then, there was a great statistical imbalance between male and female students at Oxford. Sixteen per cent were women: so, one woman to 6.25 men, that was the ratio. There was much furtive gazing in classes and lectures. Accessibility to women was enhanced by self-assurance, money and car ownership – none of which I had. Nor did I have a sister to practise on. There would be many misunderstandings ahead. The first girl I kissed at Oxford responded with the discouraging words, 'Do you think I'm a whore?' And then told me how her elder brother, a confident Wykehamist, had once shown her what kissing consisted of, by doing it on the back of her hand, shoving and squirming away with his tongue – which she, as a teenager, had found disgusting. I wasn't equipped for this sort of complication, I realised. It felt as if her brother were in the room with us. I met her occasionally down the years, but never again tried to kiss her. She may be dead now, like most of my friends from that time and place.

For the majority of students, any emotional relationship would be the first of their lives, with all the attendant gaucherie and ignorance (and sometimes without even the sex). Once a couple became established, there was a visible increase in both smugness and anxiety. There was also, in our final year, the phenomenon of 'marriage by panic': couples who'd been together for a while seeing the end of their student days approach, and suddenly getting wed. This may have looked like a pregnancy marriage (and sometimes was), but mostly the reasons were different and particular. The man, having found and retained a girlfriend against all statistical odds, didn't want his triumph to disappear; while the woman, having had her pick of this social and intellectual gene pool, feared she might not do better in the outside world. Such anxieties were never voiced, and in most cases not even entertained, by the participants; all was swept away in a cheerful, optimistic rush. And of course they loved one another, and always would, to the end of their days; and sometimes, this was even the case. On the other hand, I remember one such male student introducing his partner with the words, 'And this is my first wife.' It had seemed witty and sophisticated at the time.

Somewhere in my house, among the accumulation of necessary clutter, there are two college photographs from that time. I remember the photographer explaining to us, as we stood on tiered planking in a grey courtyard, that he would take two pictures: one serious, formal exposure (to show our families, presumably) and one in which we were allowed to 'muck around', if we wanted to. What counted as 'mucking around' was very mild stuff: lighting a cigarette, putting on a straw boater or false moustache, pulling silly faces, and so on. One group of students had brought along a six-foot cardboard cut-out of a tiger – liberated from some petrol station, where it would have been part of that long-lived Esso advertising campaign: 'Put a Tiger in Your Tank'. Some students pointed to non-existent objects in the sky; others shielded their eyes from the equally non-existent sun. In comparing the two photographs, I see that I look friendly-bored in the 'formal' one, and friendly-disapproving (a subtle, if not unobservable change) in the 'mucking about' one. Whereas Stephen, standing a few feet away, looks exactly the same in each photo: present, yet somehow withheld; observing, but neither approving nor disapproving. Making him look the only grown-up in three tiers of gurning lads.

Another sudden memory from back then. In my first year, an American friend, Priscilla, came to visit me. There were strict rules about the hours women were allowed into the college. And we both realised, as the evening in my room wore on, that she was going to break those rules, and didn't seem to mind. As the man, and the host, I was supposed to be in charge. This was not my forte. But I recognised that the problem would come in the morning. My 'scout' (a middle-aged man who cleaned my room, brought me milk, and so on) would be arriving at, say, half-past eight or nine o'clock. And women were not allowed to enter the college before ten, perhaps even eleven. And if a woman was found in a man's room, he would be sent down for a term, or maybe a year – this was well documented.

As the one in charge, I realised that Priscilla would have to hide, and the only place available would be the wardrobe. But there was a further problem. She was wearing a fairly strong scent, which would immediately be noticed by my scout as he entered my bedsitter. I decided that the only smell strong enough to disguise it (and which I could produce from available sources at the time) would be that of burnt toast. So, at some point before daybreak, I dug out my packet of sliced bread, turned my single-bar electric fire on its back, and proceeded to blacken several rounds of toast. I tossed them into the waste-paper basket, and returned to my narrow bed, where we had been far too anxious for desire to play its part. And in the morning, about an hour before my scout was due to arrive, I put Priscilla in the wardrobe (presumably with any effects she had brought) and retired back to bed.

Eventually, the scout knocked and entered. 'Oh, Fred,' I said in a languid voice, 'I'm going to have a lie-in today.' He was by now smelling a mixture of burnt toast and female perfume, plus a large rat – which he had doubtless smelt many times before. 'I want you out of there in forty minutes,' he replied sternly. Maybe he said twenty, maybe thirty; anyway, it would leave us far short of the time of day when the presence of a woman was permitted. Oh shit, I thought. I can't remember whether I got Priscilla out of the wardrobe at that stage or not. But Fred – who perhaps had a dilemma of his own in my regard – did not reappear, and a few minutes after Priscilla became legal, I walked her to the college's main gate.

But you can see how fucked up we were, even if I now had a Tale to Tell?

Strangely (to me now, less to me then) Priscilla and I never did consummate our relationship. Many years later, I was on book tour in America and a woman asked to see me for a few minutes before my event. She turned out to be Priscilla's sister, who told me that Priscilla had died about ten years previously. She added that her sister had always spoken well of me. Which came as a great surprise, as I had always felt guilty about her, because . . . but this isn't about me and her, this is just sociosexual background.

Stephen and Jean.

Oh yes, another thing. Drugs. The 1960s, as everyone knows, was the decade of Sex and Drugs. But the first was much more logistically and psychologically complicated than it is now; while the second were, to me, invisible. There was one student in my college who talked knowingly of 'Big H' and 'Little H' – which it took me a while to work out – but in those four prime years of the decade, 1964 to 1968, I was never offered so much as a reefer. The normal drugs were alcohol and cigarettes. I didn't smoke, and didn't much like alcohol. Beer tasted nasty and I rarely bought a bottle of wine.

Stephen and Jean.

Another thing. I suppose, if I were more Proustian, the smell of burnt toast might always remind me of Priscilla in the wardrobe. But it never has. And as it happens, about twenty and more years ago, I lost much of my sense of smell, which ruled out most possible Madeleine Moments. I need to put my nose deep into a flower head or a glass of wine to smell anything. Oddly, burnt toast is one thing I can smell easily, even from upstairs. But it means no more to me than the smell of burnt toast. And I am grateful it doesn't set off a 'cascade' of IAMs, recalling to me all the occasions when toast has been burnt in my presence, one after the other after the other.

Stephen was – is – was – tall and gangling. His trousers often seemed too short for him, flesh showing above his socks, and when he threw his arms about he appeared to be heading off in different directions at the same time. He owned two black jackets, two pairs of grey trousers, and a lot of white shirts. This was his outfit. We used to joke about buying him flower-power shirts and a pair of bell-bottoms. But the transformation wouldn't have worked, even as irony.

His interior was at odds with his exterior. He was soft-spoken, cautious, never threw arguments around as he did his limbs, and very attentive. No, better than that, attend*ing*. He really listened to what was being said, regardless of who was talking. Even bores might have something of use to him.

Like me, he was a scholarship boy of middle-class background. Unlike me, he knew where he was going. He was studying philosophy to make his brain orderly for a future career in either the civil service or management. Whereas I was studying it because of some spindly notion that it would make me a more serious person, teach me both how to think and how to live. Stephen would often explain to me theories and propositions which I couldn't get my head around. He was patient, and kind. He didn't have any *fantaisie* about him, but few of my friends did back then. And neither did I, for that matter.

Jean I had met when I was studying Russian. She came from a slightly posher and more rackety background than either Stephen or me. Her parents were separated, her father had a mistress, and there were frequent rows at home (we never had rows in my family, nor did Stephen in his); things were often on edge, and so was Jean. She was – what adjective might we have used back then – perhaps 'buzzy'? No, that sounds a word for an older person. Dashing? Too 1920s. Sparky, fizzy, impulsive? Feisty? Those are a bit closer, but still approximate. We got on well, partly because I half-acknowledged that she was out of my league. She headed straight towards things, and ideas, and people; she took them on, rather than being taken on herself – does that make sense? And she wanted to see the world. She'd already been to Spain and Italy and Morocco, and was planning a trip to Russia – not so easy in those days. She smoked, drank a lot of white wine, and was quite flirty. Given the 1:6.25 ratio of women to men, she was bound to have a good time, or at least the appearance of one. Her hair was between blonde and corn-coloured, with the faintest tinge of red. A natural tinge, of course; no one dyed their hair back then, not even grown-ups, as it seemed to me. Apart from women like Diana Dors and Marilyn Monroe, who didn't count. Maybe

Jean's father's mistress dyed her hair – that was the sort of thing mistresses were supposed to do. But I never met her.

I introduced them in what we liked to think of as a workers' caff in the covered market. Here they served bacon sandwiches and tea in china mugs. But there were also rock cakes and tea in cups and saucers. And if there were any market porters who ate there, they were long gone by the time we indolent students turned up – women and their shopping were the more typical clientele. Anyway, Jean and I were having coffee one morning when Stephen came past. I introduced them by describing each to the other in a semi-comic way, and Stephen joined us without any false hesitation. Two men and one woman: where were the missing 4.25 to make up the ratio? I imagined going into the caff one morning and shouting, 'Table for seven and a quarter, please.' But of course I never did.

Back then, we – by which I mean young men who, like Stephen and me, had been educated in a single-sex way – retained many primitive and theoretical ideas about women. (What about Priscilla, you may ask. And I remember that she once gave me a book on female psychology with a dedication in her American hand: 'For Julian, who never had a sister.') And because we lacked self-confidence, we sweated self-pity and anticipated rejection, while failing to imagine that girls might feel something similar at the same time. I read recently that brain development is considerably slower in boys than girls. The female cerebellum reaches its full size at eleven, while the male equivalent not until the great age of fifteen. That surely explains a few things, doesn't it, about the ways boys behave? And, as the child is father to the man, about how men behave as well.

There were other dispiriting factors. Some girls were more interested in books than in boys. Others had already met boys who were older and suaver than we were. Others again (whether by intuition or social conditioning) knew what it was they were after, and knew immediately that we were not it. Some students – for instance, those who hung around the theatre – seemed to find it easier to acquire partners than we did; sexual partners, more to the point. We explained this logically to one another: acting was all about pretending to be someone else, so they were just pretending to be more attractive and interesting than they actually were. This meant that their relationships were doomed to failure. Unless, of course, the couple each believed in the other's facade as an indicator of depth, and so stayed together. All of which made us feel superior. We assured one another that we, at least, had authenticity. Authenticity and loneliness.

This is a rough outline of how things generally were. So when Stephen and Jean got together, those who knew them felt a pleasure which excluded envy, a sort of romanticism-by-proxy. Largely, because they were so sweet together, in a 'he carried her books' kind of way. No, that's patronising, even cynical. And while we deployed cynicism in the face of public affairs – class, society, religion, politics – we – or at least I – felt none about those things that were truly important: personal relationships and art. I (or we) held those matters sacrosanct, and if we found some human relationships, as exemplified by our parents and their friends, less than holy, we were highly idealistic about our own. What was a new generation for, except to reinvent the world?

I knew the two of them for about eighteen months at Oxford, and then, weirdly, for about the same amount of time forty years later. As I said, I kept few notes on my early life, or the lives of others. And on the whole we remember less well those we count on never seeing again. So my mind's account of them back then amounts to a chaplet of moments and images, worn away like rosary beads. Walking past a late-night launderette and seeing them each with a book on their lap, doing a weekly wash together (and feeling too shy to disturb them); appraising them all togged up for some formal dinner or ball, Stephen in a rented DJ which fitted him better than his own clothes, Jean in a long royal-blue velvet dress with frills at the shoulders and a string of pearls around her neck (this is one of the sad truths of life back then: when we dressed up, we looked less like maturer versions of ourselves, and more like younger, imperfect copies of our parents); the two of them having tea in my room, where there were only two chairs, and Jean sitting on the floor with her back to Stephen's legs, which might sound subservient but was a place from which she dominated; a sudden misunderstanding between them, which had each coming to me in tears, to see if I knew something and/or could sort it all out (I didn't, and couldn't, though felt strange pride in being consulted) – but then in a few days which felt like weeks the matter, whose nature I forget, was resolved; the two of them on a bench under a peeling plane tree, revising for Finals, deeply together yet inevitably apart, given that neither could understand the other's subject. And then, most resoundingly, Stephen coming to confide in me ('She's all I've ever wanted, and all I'll ever want', a statement beyond my bounds of competence or response, except to nod pseudo-wisely), and Jean doing much the same ('I love him, but he's so *young*') – even though they both were the same age, as I boldly pointed out.

But only a few weeks later they each came to see me, after we had all done our Finals and were goofing around, getting drunk, throwing up and fearfully imagining the future out there in the stupid adult world of compromise and self-deception. Stephen, gloomy in one of his funereal black suits, saying, 'I'm afraid it's reached the point where we either marry or split.' Two days later, there was Jean, 'smiling bravely' as they put it in books, and eventually spilling out the same words: 'I'm afraid it's reached the point where we either marry or split.' I thought this an extraordinary coincidence, until I realised it must have been a form of words agreed between the two of them, a diplomatic communiqué, a telegram from that insincere world the rest of us were about to enter. I didn't understand – I didn't *want* to understand – so I mildly suggested, 'Can't you try something in between?' which was dismissed as a failure to comprehend.

I had been on the side of them getting married, because no one else I knew was anywhere near that stage, and thought it would feel a nice, bold move, not conventional at all but rather its opposite, iconoclastic. Furthermore, I could be their best man, comically fumbling for the ring and making a speech full of wit and sexual innuendo; though I didn't confess these solipsistic desires. But I also thought that our continuance as friends would be almost as good for me as for them – a state of naive benignity broken when it became clear that their original choice didn't contain the middle option I had suggested, and they had indeed, properly, split. And because I had invested far more than I was aware in their relationship, I felt betrayed; I too had been rejected and no longer had a function. Then Jean went off to do research into someone like Gogol, and Stephen took a series of part-time jobs while preparing for the civil service exams, and I got on with my own life very slowly. The first change was that I acquired a girlfriend, and found myself happy not to have to introduce her to Stephen and Jean because – how can I explain this? – their relationship had somehow become tainted in my mind, and I didn't want my new relationship to catch the taint. Does that make any sense? (It did then.) And when she and I in turn decided to split, we did so with the same assumption of continuing friendship, and we went on seeing one another for several years. In the meantime, after a few, friendly postcards, I lost contact with both Stephen and Jean, and felt hurt again, and self-righteous, indeed morally superior; an emotion which found expression in the old words, 'Oh well, in that case, fuck off wherever.'

And so they departed from one another, and also, largely, from my mind.

Years later, that first girl I kissed at Oxford, who had asked, 'Do you think I'm a whore?', and with whom I stayed in intermittent touch, told me of a subsequent lover she had in Oxford – a man I knew slightly, and someone, obviously, who *didn't* make her feel mistaken for a whore. She told me that every time they went to bed together, he would first put on a Beethoven string quartet – always the same one. I think it was opus 131, but it might have been opus 127.

I wish I had been able to ask her if, in later years, when she heard that quartet again, on the radio, say, it reminded her of their lovemaking – whether she avoided the piece, thrilled to it, or was simply indifferent. Did she blush, feel her body tense up, or smile indulgently at her earlier self? But perhaps those chords no more evoked her ex-lover than the smell of burnt toast evoked Priscilla for me. Life and memory can be so . . . quixotic, don't you find?

3
MANAGEABLE

I was lying on my front with my trousers half-loosened, as the registrar prepared for a bone-marrow biopsy. There were several pricks of local anaesthetic, then what felt more like a continual hard pressing rather than any kind of drilling on what they told me was my pelvic crest. We chatted, as I like doctors to tell me exactly what they're doing. After a while, I said,

'So I suppose this isn't curable?'

'No,' she replied straightforwardly. 'It isn't curable, but it is manageable.'

It would be managed first by drawing a fair amount of blood from me, and then by chemotheraphy – not being hooked up to a drip, but in daily, oral form. Until the condition stabilises? I asked. No, for the rest of your life. That's what 'manageable' means. The condition will accompany you to your death. It probably won't kill you, unless there is a further mutation. But otherwise you shall die with, rather than of, the condition.

She told me that the biopsy had gone well and she had several good-looking strands (if that was the word), whose content would decide exactly which kind of blood cancer I had. Would I like to see them? – she sounded pleased, indeed proud, of her handiwork. I declined. I want to know what is happening, and why, and how, but I don't want to witness everything. I avoid the needle going into the vein, the scalpel descending towards the eyelid, the catheter being inserted (and extracted), stitches put in here and there, a big toenail being lifted from its moorings, and now the laid-out juicy product which lives inside my bones and is suddenly misbehaving.

It had started in a roundabout way which puzzled various doctors. This shouldn't be a surprise. There are only about five hundred cases a year of myeloproliferative neoplasm in the country, so the average GP never sees one. Most show up when testing is done for something else. One summer and autumn I had a violent skin condition, which expressed itself in two ways: large, angry swathes on my legs, some of which eventually peeled off; and hundreds of small, hard raised spots on my back. I saw a consultant dermatologist; she was unsure of what it was, and prescribed steroid cream. Next she suggested a biopsy, which produced no answers, but left me with two neat white crosses on the inside of a wrist as reminders. Finally, she asked if I would attend a special clinic for complex or recalcitrant cases. So one morning I sat in my underpants for an hour or two in a consulting room at St George's Tooting while thirty or forty professional and trainee dermatologists inspected me and asked many of the same questions. None of them had any explanations or suggestions, apart from an elderly, bad-tempered consultant who gave me a cursory glance and said, 'It's obviously eczema, don't know what all the fuss is about.' Which made me feel a little less interesting. I didn't tell him – because she had not yet told me – that my partner Rachel, armed with photographs of my back, had gone on Google and discovered that one possible explanation of my skin condition was cancer.

There are other marks of stitching here and there on my body. But after you get to a certain age, you should expect it to bear the signs and scars of your long living; also, that most of your orifices will, one by one, have been medically invaded: ears, nose, throat, eyes (with lasers), bum, cock, vagina.

There had been another bum-invasion not long after my

dermatological adventures in Tooting. I seemed to be peeing in the night more frequently, so asked my GP if he would check my prostate. I hadn't had one of these inspections for about fifteen years. My GP (who is only a few years younger than me) agreed, but before going ahead was obliged by medical law or ethics to ask me if I would like to have an observer present. I laughed, while respecting the gesture. He then rummaged around with a latexed finger – which felt like two or three – before pronouncing: 'Well, I'm virtually certain you haven't got prostate cancer. But you can take a blood test if you want to.' There was no suggestion of either necessity or urgency, but I thought it was worthwhile. He told me of certain preconditions: for instance, you shouldn't have the test within seventy-two hours of sexual activity.

I left it ten days and gave my sample on a Thursday. On the Friday, R's sister was getting married at two o'clock. But at nine-thirty I got a call from the surgery: not from my regular GP but another doctor. He sounded halfway between anxious and alarmed. 'I haven't got the result of the prostate part of your test. But I want you to go straight to your nearest A&E and tell them you have a potassium reading of 6.5.' I had no knowledge of what this might represent, but took a briefcase with what I assumed were the usual necessities for this kind of event: chocolate, an apple, the morning's *Guardian* for the crossword, a notebook and my iPhone. Then I put on my walking boots and set off for the hospital. These were very early Covid times – lockdown was just over three weeks away, and the government, despite all the evidence from Italy, was still being insouciant, keen to defend the Englishman's sacred right to go to the pub and infect others. The A&E waiting area was full of elderly people coughing into scarves and masks. (I, of course, was also 'elderly', but not coughing made me feel younger.) I was given a blood test, and then another one. The results were perplexing: the potassium reading varied between a normal 4.4 and (as I slowly understood) a potentially life-threatening 6.5. Heart monitors were applied to my chest.

After an hour or more, an A&E doctor came to collect me. 'As soon as I saw your name, I grabbed you,' she said – which made me glad the hospital was in bookish Hampstead. She told me that she lived next door to John le Carré; we discussed him, and then she asked about my writing. It was a bit like doing a book event, if with an audience of one, who all the time was attending to her computer. Then, after a pause, she gave me a kind of answer: 'Well, I can't say if it is or isn't leukaemia.' My immediate thought was, 'Ah, so *this* is what it's like to be told.' But – to my own surprise – I was quite calm. It was, at the very least, interesting. I assumed that 'is or isn't' meant that it probably was. Or might still be so, if in the longer term. I remembered that the first time leukaemia came to my awareness was with the death of Kay Kendall, a 'glamorous redhead' as she was described back then, who featured in films with Kenneth More – there was that one about the London to Brighton rally . . .

I asked about the inconsistent potassium readings, and their meaning. They – the reason that I was there – weren't in fact significant; indeed my levels were quite normal. But what happens, if you have something that might or might not be leukaemia, is that abnormally high readings for the blood (red cells, platelets) confuse the machine into thinking your potassium levels are extremely high too. This, at least, is as I recall it.

Eventually, someone came and said, 'I think we'll take you over to the other side.' I didn't know this phrase: it seemed to come from one of those 1940s American movies in which, say, an angel disguised in gentleman's pinstripes takes the protagonist either up to heaven or – if they are already there – back down to earth to show how things are turning out. I followed someone down long corridors and was shown into a room directly opposite the nurses' station. I took off my walking boots and climbed on to the bed. It felt unnatural – it was two or three in the afternoon. I wasn't expected to get *into* the bed, was I? People came and went; more monitors were attached to my chest; my pulse was taken regularly. I was asked if I wanted to put any valuables into the safe. No, I'd rather hang on to my wallet, the only valuable I had ('except my life, except my life . . .'). I did the *Guardian* crossword.

Around five o'clock another new person came and said, 'We're sending you home, there's no point keeping you as haematology doesn't work at the weekends.' And so, without ever realising that I had been formally admitted to hospital, I was released.

Meanwhile, in another part of London, as they say . . . I hadn't been able to get a signal on my iPhone inside the hospital, but at one point had gone outside and managed to speak to R. I told her my potassium level was 6.5 and that was all they knew so far – they would be doing further tests. After which there was radio silence from me. She set off for the wedding of her sister, who was, as it happens, the head of A&E at another London hospital. Among the guests were a large number of doctors, including the head of A&E at the very hospital where I was now an inpatient; also, the head of the whole hospital. News apparently spread of my potassium count (even as it was being dismissed where I was), and as the afternoon and evening progressed, and drink was taken, and the ABBA-themed entertainment started up, a doctor who had always fancied Rachel would whisper, as she passed her chair, 'That's a *really* high potassium reading,' and then, a bit later, 'Six point five, hmmm . . .' and then, finally, 'I'll be waiting for you.' When told, I found this to be exactly how I would expect doctors (or, indeed, normal people) to behave in such circumstances. If A&E doctors can't be allowed gallows humour, who can?

Three weeks after this, I met my consultant haematologist, the approximate diagnosis was given, a pint of blood was taken straightaway, followed by the bone-marrow biopsy. Three days later, lockdown began, and so two forms of stasis were applied to my life at exactly the same moment: being obliged to stay at home, and being obliged to 'manage' my blood cancer. I was lucky in that a few months previously, I had tentatively started writing a novel, whose presence and expectations would, I hoped, keep me in one way stable. My local bookseller reported that customers were laying in copies of those long and famous novels that they'd never previously 'got around to': *Ulysses*, *War and Peace*, *Middlemarch* . . . I was dubious about this tactic, and bet him they'd be back again soon, asking for some nice short books: I felt sure that the weird stresses of lockdown would make long periods of concentration harder. In my own case, I had prepared for its first months by ordering a thirty-DVD box set of Ingmar Bergman films. Some friends though this a bit weird, if not actively morbid: 'That'll be a bundle of laughs.' I protested that Bergman was underrated as a humorist. I didn't add that great art is always consolatory. The box set arrived and contained a number of films I'd never seen, and some I'd never even heard of. But their tone was set early: the first film was called *Torment*, and the second, *Crisis*.

I have had a lifelong engagement with death, both theoretical and actual, and have written about it many times. Yet, despite the shiver of 'I can't tell if it is or isn't leukaemia', I hadn't received a death sentence. Instead, I had received a life sentence: sentenced to live with my cancer until I died. When I checked – you have to check – whether there was a possibility in my lifetime that some kind of genetic re-engineering might be able to fix my berserk bone marrow, I was told (if in more scientific terminology): fat chance. As a cheerful pessimist, I tend to look for the upside of things; but missing an ABBA-themed wedding didn't seem much to put in the balance against a cancer diagnosis.

In those first months, I had a dozen or so pints of blood drained out of me. (I asked what they did with it; they told me they poured it away – the first pint was technically reusable, but not economically so.) Gradually, my numbers came down, and I got used to the regular blood tests and reports from my consultant. I often felt tired, sometimes very tired – I might sleep for eleven hours, and then take a nap in the afternoon. But it no longer interested me to know exactly why: cancer, chemo, simple age, or a combination of all three. And I was quietly determined that the doctor at the wedding who promised to wait for R would have to wait as long as possible. Though 'determined' is the wrong word in a way, as it implies that willpower might be a factor in the outcome. This isn't the case. Mental attitudes – contrary to what we would like to believe – make no difference to cancer outcomes. 'Being brave', or being shit-scared, or occupying a midpoint of stubborn self-deception don't alter anything. The obituarial line 'He died after a long struggle with cancer, bravely borne', should read: 'He died after cancer had a long, brave struggle with him.'

I wrote the above from memory, or rather what a combination of original memory plus constant retelling had turned it into. And it's not untrue. But looking at the five pages of notes I made while in the hospital, I found the following items which I had either forgotten or eliminated:

1) They told me in A&E that my potassium count of 6.5 was almost certainly a false reading. The true reading was 4.4, which was absolutely fine (indeed, normal). The first sample must have been boiled or contaminated in some way. But just to be on the safe side, they would retest me, and if it came out at 4.4 again, they would send me home. At which point I wrote in my notebook: 'Oh dear – this may be end of story – I was hoping for something worth recording without being fatal.' Which reads like a serious temptation of the gods.
2) The A&E doctor who had some of my books on her shelves and lived next door to John le Carré told me early on that she wanted 'to protect my brain', which I now find even more touching than I did at the time. She sent me for an ECG of which I noted: 'Uninteresting.' She also said, 'I don't want to get this wrong,' which showed proper anxiety and were not words I had heard from a doctor's mouth before. She explained that my bone marrow was 'exuberantly' over-producing red blood cells and platelets, an adverb I found noteworthy. And her conclusion at this point wasn't 'Well, I can't say if it is or isn't leukaemia,' which sounds slightly cavalier; rather, it was 'I'm not in a position to say if it is or isn't leukaemia,' which is much more of a precise medical statement. And when I noted that I felt quite calm through it all, I added, 'The Canadian doctor looks much more worried (which

can't be a good sign).' She subsequently brought me a cheese roll and a bar of chocolate, and wouldn't accept repayment.

3) I wasn't put on a bed, but rather on a trolley. 'New things attached to my chest, and a fingerclip. Now I am given a call button "in case you need us". Hmm, this is getting more interesting.'
4) 'On the ceiling of the room where I am [opposite the nurses' station] there is a backlit colour photo, about 4ft x 2, of a blue sky with white fluffy clouds. That'll cheer me up. And on the left-hand wall, a photo-mural of Camden Town Underground station.'
5) The reason I was sent to A&E was that high potassium levels can lead to 'heart arrhythmia'. Which I suppose was a slight euphemism for a heart attack. (I remember doctors calling a brain tumour a 'lesion', which is a slightly less scary word, inviting the patient to ask the question only if he or she really wants to know. Whereas 'tumour' is bluntly unavoidable.) 'So now they're not worrying about that, only the high platelet level (1,000 instead of 500).' There is 'much abdominal probing and chest-pressing – nothing hurts. This means it is less likely to be leukaemia, with which there is bone pain.'
6) One of my final notes is: 'I nearly finish the crossword. But can there be a phrase YEOMAN'S SARDINE? Another blood test. Asked: "Do you live alone?" "Yes." Then, "Do you have a carer?" I laugh [so much] that she [the nurse] says, "I won't ask you the others then . . ." which are probably, "Do you have a colostomy bag?" and so on.'

In the interregnum between 'I'm not in a position to say if it is or isn't leukaemia' and a definitive diagnosis – when I knew that I 'merely' had some kind of blood cancer – I naturally started making notes for what would be my final book, finished or unfinished. Most people, I assume, have imagined this situation, and what their response might be. Mine consisted of a single item: Write it down. So, on 24 March 2020, the day the country was locking down for Covid, I wrote the provisional (provisionally awful, and archly self-pitying) title of '*Jules Was*' on a fresh page of my notebook. The draft only reached two and a half pages. Here are some of the entries:

– This is the start of the ending.
– I live in the present, but my future is to exist only in the past.
– Knowing that I had a partner, the consultant asked if we intended having any – any more? – children. 'No,' I said, explaining that R was postmenopausal and already had two of her own. 'Because,' he went on, dutifully finishing the thought, 'we wouldn't recommend it and would advise barrier protection.'
– The postman, wearing black gloves, rings the bell and leaves two parcels on the step. 'It's what we've been told.' The newspapers won't be delivered after today. The British have stocked up on lavatory paper, hand sanitiser, and soap; also dried pasta and tinned tomatoes. We are two weeks behind Italy whose death toll is painful to follow.
– The writer, quarantined in his own home, suddenly victim of blood cancer, while all around a plague is spreading exponentially. It sounds like a bad, or at least derivative, novel. And yet there are promising themes.

Thus: he is meticulous about self-isolation because he doesn't want to die of coronavirus. He would much rather die of blood cancer. It is not just the timescale of it – three weeks to a strangulating Covid death, which is very nasty to watch, let alone suffer, according to A&E specialists. He would rather die of his own disease, thank you very much, not everybody else's.

– And, without yet knowing its ramifications, or the nature of its end, he prefers to have blood cancer. Is this snobbery? A little. He doesn't want lung, or liver, or bum, or whatever; doesn't want bits of him chopped off or out. It feels a more private, personal form of cancer. Whether it will feel like this as it progresses is anyone's guess. And he will still be a carcass at the end of it. Assuming the virus doesn't get him first.

– The Dutch prime minister assures his people that they do not need to hoard lavatory paper as the country has a six-year supply of it. The Germans are working on a vaccine which may be more advanced than others. There is cross-border co-operation in Europe on medical matters. And we have left – effectively if not yet legally.

– Also, it's not the sort of cancer that I can feel responsible for, and therefore guilty about. Oh if only I hadn't smoked/drunk so much/eaten so much ultra-processed food . . . It's a cancer caused by the body getting old, starting to break down, and turn against its own best interests. It's a cancer rooted in the universe's utter indifference. It's random, it has no significance – it's just the universe doing its stuff. Don't insert morality or purpose into its unrolling and denouement.

- Brian M[oore] said he hoped he wouldn't die in the middle of a novel 'in case some other bastard came along and finished it for me'. I am not in the middle of anything – a tiny start on the Pale Galilean novel, but I was starting it too soon anyway.
- Kersti, my friend of half a century, now eighty-eight herself, and living alone, is already in semi-isolation, but has been self-isolating much more, and not going out at all. Why? Because of a TV programme in which it was explained how, when the crisis peaks and equipment is inadequate, doctors will have to decide who should be given a chance of living, and who must go straight to 'end-of-life care'. Weeping, K says that she didn't want to put anyone through that moral decision on her behalf. No one is a saint, but she has many saintly aspects.
- Writing this – at the time of writing – makes me calm. The concentration on the words, on getting it as true as I can. This was the same when Pat [my wife] was dying. Terror and anguish were kept away by writing about terror and anguish, which came when I was not writing. I am also calm in hospital – it is a necessary business we are about, and the best way is to be clear-minded and clear-hearted.
- My diary has blank weeks and cancellation lines through dinners, concerts, operas, outings. And whereas RFH used to mean Royal Festival Hall, now it means Royal Free Hospital.

There are two side-notes to these notes. One reads 'triage fantasy – badge'. In these first days of Covid I was, like my friend Kersti, pre-haunted by the notion of exhausted doctors being forced to make quick decisions about who should live and who should die. I imagined myself being rushed to hospital, breathless, speechless, perhaps even unconscious. They see this old geezer and are coming down on the side of straight to 'end-of-life care' when one of them notices that I am wearing a lapel badge. It reads: BUT I WON THE BOOKER PRIZE. And I am reprieved. Unless the gesture looks like an attempt to pull rank, in which case . . . well, I would never find out.

The second note reads 'Brain racing at night' and then a reference to my friend Terence Kilmartin, literary editor of the *Observer* for more than thirty years. As clever as he was modest, Terry combined this job with the minor pastime of retranslating the whole of Proust's *À la Recherche*. He had prostate cancer in his early sixties, a remission of some years, then cancer returned to his bones and brain. He rang up late one evening, his brain racing, with one thought, which was to deprioritise himself. 'It's much worse for Joanna [his wife].' I found this incomprehensible, and said to myself, 'But Terry's *dying*.' What could be worse?

Terry died in 1991. Seventeen years later, I understood what he meant, when Pat died. All deaths inflict collateral damage. The dying person will soon feel nothing, while the griefstruck will be irradiated for years to come. Yes, I could see why Terry said, 'It's worse for Joanna,' even while I stubbornly insist that it was and is worse for him. 'But having been in Joanna's position and fully experienced grief, I now think I have the easier job, which is to die (and I trust I'll get a little help with that). What I am, not most, but heavily afraid of, is the grief I shall impose on R.'

But this draft went no further as the haematologist confirmed my luck of the draw. I subsequently learnt that the name for a false potassium reading is pseudo-hyperkalaemia. And also found myself reflecting that while I had been urgently despatched to hospital with a supposed condition which might easily lead to a heart attack, I was in fact suffering from a different condition but which might also have led to the same result. Either that or a stroke. And before it was brought under control, my platelet level had risen from 1,000 to 1,600.

The day after I had been admitted and discharged from the Royal Free Hospital, I looked up the answers to the previous day's *Guardian* crossword. And of course there was no such phrase as YEOMAN'S SARDINE. It was YEOMAN'S SERVICE.

There is the account of my blood cancer I gave at the start of this section, written from memory. There are the scribbled notes I made in hospital, and the brief, alarmed text of '*Jules Was*'. And then there is the main contemporaneous account, the formally informal one of my diary. I have kept a diary for over half a century, and it is, like all diaries, fully partial. And like most diaries, it aims to tell truths that cannot be expressed elsewhere. But happy times tend to expend themselves in the moment; whereas unhappy, bleak, mendacious, envious, petty times are generally suppressed, only to flood the diary later with sadness, rage and self-pity. Rereading some early portions, I wonder: was I really like that? And for how much of the time? I thought I was a genial, friendly and laughing young man. And I was that too.

I don't note individual days or months in my diary, just the start of each new year. I type it up more or less as it happens and stick the pages into a hardbound A4 notebook, typically of 192 pages. As I fill only the recto side of the paper, that makes ninety-six pages per volume. I am now on vol. 18. If each page contains roughly 450 words, this makes about 777,000 words. That figure, coming up just now on my ancient pocket calculator, seems daunting. The longer you live, the more monomaniacal you appear.

One entry on the first page for 2020 reads: 'I was feeling sorry for myself in a cab coming home in the rain and dark the other day: Bad Foot day, allergic rash returned on body, prostate sub-alarm . . . and then I see a young blind Chinese guy coming towards me [on the pavement] on the arm of a young carer, seemingly headed for a burger bar. Then, as the cab advanced, I saw that behind the blind Chinese guy was another, holding on to the first one's shoulder, and behind him another, and behind him another . . . yup, count your fucking blessings, mate.'

I think I always have tried to count my (non-theological) blessings, not in a Little Mary Sunshine kind of way, but soberly, observing them in the context of life's finitude. But neither happiness nor misery are controllable. Joyfulness, pleasure, passionate interest – like their photographic negatives, sadness, grief and boredom – flow over us in waves. We can take precautionary measures, seeking to prolong the former and delay the latter, but these make only a minor difference. At least, it seems to me that this is the case, assuming that you want to learn and admit the truth about life, and the truth about yourself. If you choose to look away, pretend to a cheerfulness and even happiness that you don't authentically feel, this can work to some extent. If everyone around you agrees they are happy, perhaps you are too, because there are no real tests for happiness except the assertion of the individual concerned. Further, happiness can be social. There is satisfaction in observing the rules and habits of the tribe, and for some people this works, despite their not essentially believing in those rules and habits; even self-sacrifice can instil a kind of happiness.

For instance, I recently read *The Loved and the Unloved* by François Mauriac, one of my favourite French novelists, who wrote about Catholicism from the inside, and whose fiction refutes the notion that the novel is an entirely secular form. At one point, we are told about the case of a certain Mme Dubernet, who has always lived her life as the sternest of Catholics and is now dying. 'She is convinced that all is well between her and God . . . She has arranged everything down to the last detail . . . She is not worrying about God. But if she discovered that He didn't exist after all, she wouldn't show the slightest surprise. There's nothing more matter-of-fact than these old bred-in-the-bone Catholic dames.'

I go to my diary, to check the fourth and most complete version of my diagnosis and treatment, not so much out of self-absorption but as a demonstration of how memory (and record-keeping) works, and of what gets forgotten as the mind processes its vast input of 'facts' to be stored.

– When I set off for the hospital, as well as the *Guardian*, an apple and chocolate (here specified as an After Eight bar), I also took a 'printed-out piece on Huysmans I'm working on'. I can quite see why my subsequent anecdotal account suppressed this detail.
– When the nurse asked if I wanted to hand over my valuables for safekeeping, she also asked me to sign a form saying 'the hospital would not be legally responsible if anything were lost'. I think it was this clause that persuaded me not to hand over my wallet.

– 'How many people am I looked at/treated by in my seven hours or so in there? Twenty? Twenty-five? Different countries, ethnicities, etc, but it all seems to me astonishingly efficient, and, indeed, a marvel, one of the few things we can really be proud of, and I loathe Johnson, Gove, Cummings and their alt-right US backers for wanting to tear it down.'
– On that first visit to the haematology department, they didn't, as I'd remembered, take one pint of blood out of me, but two. Further, 'Two [more] pints of Barnes's Best are drained in the next ten days. My blood cancer is a combination of Essential (essential!) Thrombocythaemia and Polycythaemia Vera, two of the three sorts of myeloproliferative neoplasm (the third one you don't want to get). And by "manageable" they meant "unless there is another mutation, of which there is a five per cent chance".' So my life expectancy is not seriously compromised: 'unless, of course I get bum cancer etc etc as well. It has all been interesting: the bleedings, the blood tests, the wary camaraderie of fellow patients. I really love talking to the doctors and nurses – just as I love talking to policemen. The chemo was quite fatiguing at first . . . but the body is adjusting. But I have a sharp appetite for food, and am in bed for about ten hours most nights. And the hospital doesn't need to see me for three months, so that's a win.'
– 'Second round of being bled: this time, they take four pints in four weeks. Actually, three and three-quarters, as last week they didn't get the needle in properly, so the blood started clotting before the bag was full. My haematocrit needs bringing down. Coincidentally,

the Tour de France is on, and I remember the days of EPO, raising the red-cell count as high as possible, and young, enthusiastic cyclists overdoing it and dropping dead in the middle of the night.'

– At the start of 2021, I didn't write a word in my diary for three months. 'And yet: Cancer, Covid, Brexit . . . much to feel, little to write.' And 'While lockdown has been lowering psychologically at times . . . I am at the most coddled end of the spectrum.' Meaning that I have money, work that is normally and happily done alone, a house and garden, two parks a short distance away, one of which I walk across to the hospital for my treatments. At seventy-five I am much better off than the young, who are having a year or more of their lives stolen. The fact that the government has declared me to be in a Clinically Extremely Vulnerable category is 'almost an advantage – can't go out, shouldn't go out. Again, I could outline the inconveniences – fifteen per cent loss of energy, the bloodletting, increased memory loss – but again, it's at the lower end of cancer – no operations, no radiotherapy, just chemo in pill form until I die. I work more slowly, but I think the results are still as cogent as before. My skin-rash occasionally returns (cancer) and my toenails grow more erratically, as does my hair (chemo), and my hair needs washing every four weeks instead of every two days (lockdown plus chemo, I guess). I get hungrier than before, though my friends say I am thinner ("Cancer – great for slimmers," I reply).'

– 'My daily intake: 1 gram chemo, blood-thinner, simvastatin, amitriptyline, vitamin D oral spray.

And while I am occasionally self-pitying, I am never competitive about illness. Around this time, I went to stay with friends in the country. The other guests were all about my age, and at breakfast several of them took out their pillboxes and delved into them. Some were larger than others, but they were all dwarfed when the most alpha male among us sat down. He brought out a pillbox which looked like an architect's scale model for a 1960s tower block, with its little drawers indicating balconies. He had obviously "won" (though I did not conclude that he was actually any iller than the rest of us). Since then, I have added tamsulosin hydrochloride to my daily intake, while at weekends my chemo intake has been raised to a gram and a half.'

– An exchange with a nurse taking a blood test which I failed to write down at the time. As she was filling the two or three phials from my arm, I asked her which sort of jab she had had. 'Pfizer,' she replied instantly. 'I had AstraZeneca,' I said. After a moment, she added, 'No – I'm joking.' 'You're not vaccinated?' 'No.' 'Why?' 'I'm not convinced,' she replied. I didn't press her on whether her grounds were religious or medical or crazy-internet. 'But you do agree it exists?' I pressed. 'Yes,' she said, holding on to the tube into my arm with one hand, while making a large circle above her head with the other, 'it's all around.' I was surprised rather than alarmed by this – we were both wearing masks and close to one another for only two to three minutes. Later, I asked my consultant about this. He said that ten to twenty per cent of the staff were probably unvaccinated; the hospital can urge them to get a jab, and tries to keep them away from front-line patients, but won't and can't force them to be vaccinated. This seems entirely sensible.

– More recently, I had another exchange with a nurse and made this note in my diary: 'As the nurse is filling the usual two phials with my blood, I ask her what's the most she's ever filled. "A hundred and fifteen," she replies, "and fifty-three for the second." I am momentarily perplexed, thinking she must mean this is the most she has filled in a morning or a day's work; but no, these are indeed the figures for a single patient in one draining. Count your fucking blessings indeed.

All the same, I find myself in a medical position I had not anticipated. Normally, you have an illness, go to the doctor and/or hospital, and you are cured or not cured, or cured for a bit until the illness reappears, when again it will be cured or not cured. Whereas mine is incurable but manageable, a constant companion which needs to be fed a daily dose of chemo to keep it happy, or at least subservient. I have it, and it has me, indelibly. When first thinking seriously about death, I came up with an image for it: not as something that awaits us, a terminus at the end of a journey, an arrival from which there will be no further departure. Rather, I thought of it as always being there, on a set of parallel tracks alongside my life. And at any point some unexpected set of points might bring it swerving across my path to obliterate me. I still think of it in this way, except now there is also my blood cancer running on another set of tracks on the other side of me. And if the engine of death swerves across us, we shall be wiped out together, at exactly the same moment. I almost feel sorry for my cancer; though I must be careful not to personify it in any way. Some cancer-sufferers do this, naming their tumour after someone they most hate or despise – Boris or Thatcher or Putin or whoever. I can see the attraction of this: you have named an enemy to whom you are determined not to succumb. But as we know, this is a mental tactic which makes no difference to the outcome. And anyway, in my case, there is no centre to my illness that I can name and vilify. It's just an anonymous overall presence – not really a companion as I just called it, for it hardly feels companionable. Nor, perhaps strangely, does it ever act as a daily reminder of death. Because I don't need another prompt.

'Incurable yet manageable', that sounds like . . . life, doesn't it? Though there are, inevitably, some dreamers who attempt to evade this existential equation. They tend to be the ultra-rich, who also indulge in space travel and paranoid fantasies. For them, the way out of death's trap is to be found in extending the length of human life, reversing the process of ageing, and transporting us (though these para-dreamers will get the first seats out) to some planet where our breathing will be slowed and we shall live for much, much longer. In the meantime we trash the only planet we have, and make life unliveable for future generations.

Then there are the hopeful ones who believe in cryonics. It's not my area of expertise, though if I were you, I wouldn't rush into it. Cryonics firms take your money, freeze you, promise to reanimate you when technological advance makes that feasible, and in the meantime they live off your money, while perhaps not always paying full attention, as you have been promised, to the long term. Electricity costs go up, a director of the firm needs a cash injection, and suddenly you are all goo and bones in a deconsecrated refrigerator. And the cryonically frozen can hardly sue for negligence or breach of contract. Take the recent case of the baseball star Ted Williams, who was cryogenised by the Alcor Life Extension Foundation. 'Unfortunately, Alcor's surgeons beheaded him, drilled holes in his temples and accidentally cracked his skull ten times.' Imagine waking up with no body and a massive headache. All part of the American Dream turning sour. A friend of Edith Wharton's defined the perfect formula Hollywood was always in quest of as 'a tragedy with a happy ending'. It might work in the movies, but it doesn't work in life.

4
THE END OF THE STORY

How to tell a story with a missing middle? I've thought about this, as you may imagine. And I'd say that it may not be curable, but is at least manageable.

Most writers get letters. My wife used to say, satirically, that I became a writer 'in order to get letters'. I'd reply, or explain, that most writers (though not all) enjoy a response to their work from people other than critics and friends. My rule is to answer all courteous letters, but never give out my address. I've had one stalker in my life, and that was enough.

This letter was headed 'A Voice from the Past' and turned out to be from Stephen. He said that now he'd taken early retirement (he didn't say what from) and had more time for reading, he'd been 'catching up' on me. He then said some nice things – by which I don't mean words of praise, but rather something writers after a few years crave even more: an accurate representation of, and correct response to, something they've written. (And by 'correct' I don't necessarily mean praiseful.) He didn't suggest we meet, which was in keeping with his character as I remembered it. And I found that I missed him. Is that right? Anyway, I felt some nostalgia at the sight of his extremely careful if now somewhat looser handwriting, and some curiosity too; so I suggested we meet for a drink next time he was up in London. And he behaved properly about that too, not rushing up a few days later but getting in touch again after about six weeks. We met at the bar of a station hotel and tick-boxed our lives. Marriage, one child currently in Australia, friendly divorce for him; marriage, no children, widowhood for me.

His travelling the world for his firm; my staying at home with my typewriter. And so on.

At one point I asked him if he ever thought about Jean.

'Frequently,' he replied. And I recognised this as a true and exact response typical of him. 'All the time' I would have shied away from; 'occasionally' I would not have been intrigued by. But 'frequently' meant that he meant it.

'I wonder what's happened to her,' I said, perhaps disingenuously.

Stephen was never disingenuous, as his reply showed:

'I want you to help me meet her again.'

'I don't have her address, I've no idea where she is.'

'But I do. Her email, that is. She runs a gardening business.'

'Then why do you need me?'

'We needed you before,' he said. 'You were how we met.'

'Yes, but . . . well, we're all grown up now. Nearly pensioners and all that.'

'All the more need then.'

I paused. I was partly reflecting on the way he had said 'we' in 'We needed you before'. They weren't a 'we' now, but he spoke as if they were.

'Stephen, I think this is a really bad idea.'

'Why?'

'Never go back. Let sleeping dogs lie, and so on.'

'I didn't think you'd resort to clichés.'

'Sometimes clichés are just accumulated wisdom.'

He shook his head. 'And that's another one.' I remembered his occasional sternness with me, when I had been attempting to understand philosophy; and I liked it again now.

'Haven't you ever?' he asked.

'Ever what?'

'Gone back.'

'Yes, once or twice, after my wife died. Maybe three times.'

'And?'

'Always a bad idea. No, that's not true. Once a good idea, once a near miss, once a bad idea.'

'There you are. Anyway, this is different.'

'Why? How?'

'Because I'm not you.'

That, at least, was incontrovertible.

The Grand Reunion. Maybe I shouldn't have arranged it as I did, but it seemed like a good idea at the time, as the man said when he jumped off the bridge. But anyway, I'll leave you to be the judge. Jean was now living outside Swindon, and I would be coming down from London, so Oxford seemed enough of a mid-point. And how about . . . well, why not try to find that old workers' caff we used to go to in the covered market? And if we can't find it we'll meet at that butcher's which always used to have lots of game hanging on hooks outside? If it still exists. In any case, here's my mobile number.

And then I gave the same rendezvous, but half an hour later, to Stephen, and told him I'd text him the location, and that he was to approach the table from behind Jean, and walk past, and I wouldn't take any notice of him, and then do a further circuit. If the mood seemed inauspicious, I'd ignore him a second time, in which case we should meet again at the King's Arms an hour or so later; whereas if I judged it appropriate, I'd leap to my feet.

'You haven't changed,' I said, as Jean sat down opposite me.

'Liar,' she replied cheerfully.

'Well, I mean, in the circumstances. But no, really not.' This was awkward of me, I admit. I tried to explain about bone structure remaining the same, and eyes, and smiles, when she cut me short.

'I like some of your books but not others.'

'That's hardly surprising.'

'This hybrid stuff you do – I think it's a mistake. You should do one thing or the other.'

In the old days, I might have said, 'Well, at least you like some of my books.' Now I said, firmly: 'I don't mind you not liking my books, but you are mistaken if you think I don't know exactly what I'm up to when I write them.'

She raised an eyebrow as if I were a touchy old bugger, so I cut to the chase.

'Do you ever think about Stephen?'

'Yes.'

'And how do you think about him?'

'Fondly.'

We talked of her life between Then and Now, and her gardening business, and I avoided jokes about hybrids (maybe she liked them in flower beds) – at which point I leapt to my feet, perhaps a little melodramatically, and said, 'Talk of the devil!' And then, 'Why don't you join us?' and Stephen slid in beside Jean as he had done forty years previously. He was looking at her, but she was only looking at me, and not benignly.

'You novelist,' she said, and I could tell she was really quite angry. 'You fucking novelist, couldn't resist, could you?'

'Well,' I replied, 'I've always believed that form is as important as subject matter.'

'And now you're a smug fucking novelist! I knew there was something fishy about it all.' Then, turning to Stephen, 'You see, I swear just as much as I always did.'

He said, quietly, 'I always liked it, as you might remember.'

She smiled. 'I probably do it more now. That's what life

does to you – does to me, anyway. When do you swear, Stephen, and under what circumstances?'

I realised that, if I'd ever had control of the proceedings, I had certainly lost it now.

'Well, I do swear, yes,' he replied, 'from time to time, but only at myself, I'd say.'

'Jesus Christ, Stephen, he's turned into a fucking novelist and you've turned into a fucking saint.'

At which point, thank God, we all laughed at exactly the same moment, and it seemed as if time had concertinaed and, if only for a while, we were picking up where we had left off. No, that's not quite right: more as if we were picking up where we had first started.

And after half an hour or so, Stephen rose and said he was glad he had chanced across us, at which we all laughed again. He said he had a train to catch, which was code for 'See you in the King's Arms after you're through with Jean.' Who says novelists aren't capable of being practical in life? Or devious, if you prefer.

When she in turn got up to leave, I explained. 'What Stephen said meant I was to meet him in the King's Arms. Why don't you come along and surprise him back?'

'God, you're so damn pleased with yourself today.'

And I was. And she followed me to the King's Arms, and later, I left them there, as I had a train to catch – and yes, I really did.

When I got up, Jean said, 'You're a chancer, Mr Barnes.'

But this sounded to my ears like praise. On the train, I thought about it. Had I been a chancer in my life? Sometimes so, sometimes not. But she didn't mean that. She meant: a chancer with other people's lives. But isn't that what all novelists are, essentially? In their books, at least.

*

As we passed Reading, I thought of my own attempts at going back, and one of them in particular. She and I had known each other in a passing, friendly way years before, and this time there was more intent on both sides, but also edginess. As in edging towards one another, and as in being edgy: at times a sense of wanting to get out before you're in – do you know what I mean? Anyway, we had a lunch, and a dinner and another lunch, and I found myself remembering a red coat she had worn once – twenty years ago? More? Whereupon she fiercely replied that she had never, ever owned a red coat, and when I said I was fairly sure she had, went on, 'You're looking at me through the wrong end of a telescope.' I didn't know why I was being rebuked. Aren't you allowed to remember someone back then, and then perhaps slowly work your way towards what they are now? Apparently not. So I was edgy in response, and we called it – whatever it might have been going to be – off before it had started.

And later she admitted that, yes, she had indeed owned what I might well have assumed was a red coat, though it was in fact more of a cape.

So I found myself wondering if Stephen was viewing Jean through the wrong end of a telescope.

Proust says somewhere that 'The memories which two people preserve of one another, even in love, are not the same.' I would change that 'even' to 'especially'.

There's been quite a bit of Proust in this book, I realise. And I'm not even a Proustian. But perhaps that shows because, as above, I quote him mainly in order to disagree.

I told you that I had promised Stephen and Jean not to write about them. Actually, it was worse than that: I *swore an oath* not to do so. Swore *on a Bible* not to do so. Can you believe that, in the twenty-first century? Like some presidential oath-taking. Do you remember the first swearing-in of Donald Trump? They told him he would be handed the Bible on which countless previous presidents had sworn to uphold the constitution. He replied – Rebel, Rebel! – that he preferred to use his own Bible. (Maybe it was an ancient copy of the 'Wicked Bible', the 1631 reprint of the King James Version, in which a compositor's error turned the seventh commandment into 'Thou shalt commit adultery'. That would have been appropriate.) Anyway, there was a stand-off and it was eventually agreed he would swear on *both* Bibles to uphold the constitution, and so on. And we all saw how twice as many Bibles made him twice as virtuous in office.

So when, a few weeks before their wedding, Jean asked me to swear on a Bible that I would never write about her and Stephen, I thought she was joking. I said I'd rather swear on a copy of Emily Dickinson's poems. Or, I was going to add, the Rules of Cricket, or a bus timetable, or the most recent Labour Party manifesto. But I saw from her face that she was frighteningly serious. Well, it wasn't me who was getting married. And at the same time, I was quite impressed by her level of distrust.

I fetched a floppy-bound Bible from my study – the only copy in the entire house – blowing the dust off the top fore-edge as I did so. I wondered if she wanted me to raise it in the air as I swore, or hold it in one hand while raising the other presidentially, or place one hand on top of it and . . . No, I didn't really think any of those things, it's just that the absurdity of the situation tempts me to misremember, or rather, invent. But what I *did* think was: who, if I broke my oath, would condemn me, and to what? Would the Jehovah of the Old Testament engulf me in fire and brimstone – whatever brimstone is? Or perhaps the God of the New Testament (see Jimmy Carter and adultery) might let me off more lightly. But since neither of these monstrous figments exists – or ever has – I calculated that the chances of divine repercussion were less than zero. We come from eternal nothingness and that is what we return to. Which might affect – if not necessarily justify – the way we behave towards those already dead. Or perhaps Jean was thinking that I would be condemned by my own conscience if I broke my oath. Anyway, one atheist swore to another on a book neither of them was guided by in life that he would not do something he subsequently did.

With Stephen it was different. We were having a drink together. At one point he looked away and said quietly, 'I hope you won't ever think of writing about Jean and me.' And I replied, 'Of course not – in any case, that's not how it works.' And he replied, 'Good.' And we left it there. I didn't bother him with an explanation of the compost theory of writing. But now, in a strange way – or is it so strange? – I feel I have betrayed Stephen more than I have Jean.

I have found myself thinking a lot in recent years about how we remember the dead, about how quickly memory becomes myth and once-living people are turned into a set of anecdotes (but how could it be otherwise?). I remember a story my father liked to tell. He grew up in Derbyshire, and once, as a young man visiting home, he went to a football match. He was standing on the terrace, and the home team were playing badly, when one of their forwards, with the ball at his feet, broke towards the visitors' goal. 'Shoot, Brady!' shouted a man to my father's immediate left. Whereupon a man behind them riposted, 'Don't shoot Brady, shoot the whole fucking lot of them!'

He didn't say 'fucking', of course. My father, that is. He said 'bloody'. I never heard him use the F-word or any of its derivatives in his entire life. 'Bloody' was as far as he would go (in the presence of others, anyway). I just assume that the neighbour on the terrace said 'fucking', and it makes a minimally better story that – or if – he did. I can't remember the name of the player – 'Brady' is my necessary invention. Nor am I sure if the incident took place at the Derby County ground. Or that my father was back visiting home. It might have happened when he was a schoolboy for all I know. Or in Nottingham, where he went to university. But then I have to give a place and time when the incident took place (when? perhaps a century ago) or the exchange would lack the modest depth of an anecdote. In my view, you can fudge the background if you respect the central, fundamental truth of the story. Which I can hardly check on now. My father has been dead for thirty years, and Brady, which wasn't his name, probably for many more.

'Whatever brimstone is'. According to my dictionary, it means 'burning stone', presumably as in what was placed upon you, or onto which you were placed, by horned and betailed devils wielding pitchforks, while in the background burning lakes of the stuff simmered and belched away. But we don't believe in hell anymore, and brimstone is now the name of a butterfly – a nice moral transition. Which you might expect to be a burning red-hot stone colour, but is in fact buttercup yellow (in the case of the male – the female is a pale greenish-yellow). Which is a bit mysterious.

With hell gone, and the Tragic Age well past, our main use for hot stones nowadays is in massage therapy. Jean, in her latter years, was to become a devotee of spa treatments, and spent weekends away at hotels which offered the whole range: hot stones, cold baths, mud-encasement, and so on. I used to imagine her lying back, wrapped in a towel, with cucumber slices over her eyes.

Brimstone, I learn from a larger dictionary, was a synonym for sulphur. Which was what hell smelt of. And which was bright yellow. So the name of the butterfly is not mysterious at all. You may have noted my habit of correcting myself. When I was younger, I thought I knew what the world was like, what was true and hard, what malleable and soft. The need for self-correction comes with age, like the habit of repetition. It must have something to do with death and departure from this life. Like confessing your sins and errors in the old days. Now it's a different sort of reckoning before you die. 'I just want to get this one thing straight,' we say. As if it will make much difference, at the time, or later.

Anyway, back to Stephen and Jean, Part Two. I was absent from their courtship – their second courtship – and happily so. I had, at Stephen's prompting, stage-managed their reunion; the rest was entirely up to them. I told myself not to invest anything in what might happen; for all I knew they might even now be having an argument about whether or not she had owned a red coat forty years previously. I told them that I was working on a book, a foolproof excuse, because, in one way or another, I always am. And after four months they sent me an email – a joint one – asking me to be their best man. At a church wedding. At which point I realised that I had, after all, been investing a lot in them. The news made me happy; also, it provided a narrative arc and satisfying conclusion to a story in a way that life rarely does. Four decades previously, I had wanted to play my part in a public ceremony. Now, at long last, it was going to happen, and I would get my chance. This time, in the real version, there would be no comic juggling with the ring, no speech laced with double entendres, and no awful jokes at the bridegroom's expense.

But as it turned out, there wasn't going to be a best man's speech at all. Jean considered it far too cheesy a tradition.

In middle age, she had taken to dogs and long country walks with them. Her current dog, when she and Stephen reconnected, was a Jack Russell called Jimmy. He had been the runt of the litter, and when she first obtained him, she used to carry him around in her coat pocket. He was now nearly a year old, and probably full-grown, but still small. I don't know if you're familiar with the breed, but they are feisty, characterful dogs on the whole. Witty, too. (Can a dog be witty? Well, I have a friend whose Jack Russell, when hungry, goes to its bowl, lies down on its back and sticks its legs up in the air, simulating death. And stays in that position until notice is taken.) They are also notorious for their aggression, rage, and sudden changes of mood. Jimmy, for instance, will allow himself to be stroked along his back during the daytime, but if you stroke him there after dark, he will bite you, regardless of who you are.

The first time Stephen went over to Jean's place, a furious barking preceded her opening of the door. Through the crack, she said, 'Don't make eye contact with him.' When Stephen tried to pet him, Jimmy bit him hard on the thumb. Later, he bit his trouser bottoms and shoelaces, also pissing on a sweater foolishly discarded within dog-range. He was just defending his mistress, that much was clear and ordinary; but he was also a jealous little fucker. What, for some reason, would send him into a berserk frenzy was if he caught Stephen looming over Jean – he standing, she on the sofa, for instance – in what to the canine mind was judged a threatening manner. Like, for instance, when he brought her a cup of tea.

But Stephen persisted, accompanying them on walks, picking up Jimmy's shit, filling his dog-bowl with offcuts from the Sunday roast as a change from Turkey Rusks for Lively Dogs. Straightforward bribery, of course, but a good tactic. And slowly, Jimmy began to see the usefulness of Stephen, and realise that his largeness could be advantageous. When there was thunder and lightning, let alone fireworks, it was to Stephen that Jimmy turned, cramming up next to him between the sofa's end and a warm male thigh. And eventually he decided that his defensive duties extended to Stephen's house and garden as well as to Jean's.

I don't want to go on about Jimmy, but one of his many appealing traits was his instant alert to any possible incursion into home territory. And this didn't have to be a visible human incursion. When letters came through the door, he would intercept them in mid-fall and bite them into submission. Gas bills with multiple perforations were a normal thing for Jean. And after he had bitten the post – much better than biting the actual postman – he would trample on the letters until they gave no last sign of life and movement. Then Jimmy would retire complacently to his bed for a while.

I hadn't lived with a dog since my childhood, and Jimmy taught me various things I didn't know about canines. For instance, that the biblical phrase 'as a dog returns to its vomit' is in no way metaphorical.

You can't have a stag night in your sixties. So Stephen came round to my house for a couple of glasses of white wine. He asked me if I would be in charge of Jimmy at the church.

'They're letting Jimmy in? That's pretty risky, I'd say.'

Stephen explained that he and Jean had had a meeting with the vicar. For a start, there wasn't any problem with one of them being divorced: the Church was desperate for business nowadays. As for Jimmy's presence, Stephen asked if a small dog, famous for his good behaviour, might be allowed to accompany its mistress. He had prepared his arguments – all God's creatures and so on. Why, there are even churches offering a yearly blessing of animals, to which you can bring your spavined pony, scrofulous bunny, and so on. But the vicar, for all his subsequent faults, replied that in his experience animals were far less trouble at a service than babies.

Just before leaving, Stephen said, 'It's wonderful. I know I'm doing the right thing. It's not like the first time, it's so much richer now. This is where I am. Where I always should have been.'

After he had gone, Jean texted me. 'Incredibly nervous. You might have to hold my hand, Jx.'

I replied, 'Of course. Seems quite normal anyway. Anxiety, I mean. Though also hand-holding.'

(Did I tell you that Jean and I once went to bed together? Yes, I thought that might come as a surprise. And inevitably, it burst into my head with all the force of an involuntary autobiographical memory as I was double-checking that I had the ring safely in my pocket. It happened towards the end of our final year. One of those studenty things, you could say. She was sharing a flat with two other girls who had gone home for the weekend. And I was round there. I don't know where Stephen was. And we ended up in bed together. But it didn't work out. I found I couldn't, or wouldn't – the margin is often fine. Not that I was too drunk, I didn't have that excuse. 'I think it's because I like you too much,' I said. The lights were out, and she replied, 'Or not enough.' Which wasn't the case, but a fair riposte in the circumstances. In a way it was a relief to both of us – we hadn't betrayed Stephen. Though of course we had. And to compound it, we stayed in her cramped single bed all through the night. I lay awake, thinking how some bad things could be good. Or the other way round. And we never referred to it again. It wasn't taboo, just something we didn't mention. And I'm pretty sure she never told Stephen, because on the day of the Bible-swearing, Jean included all mention of 'that night' in my vow's terms of reference.)

I was a bit surprised they had a church wedding. Stephen said it was Jean's decision. Jean said she could tell it was what Stephen wanted, even if he couldn't articulate it. Both said it was more for the pleasure of others than for themselves. Most people, they said, wanted 'a proper ceremony, something to remember'. But not, of course, one with that old bullshit about the woman promising to obey, and the man promising to endow her with all his worldly goods. It was to be a post-serious wedding, if you know what I mean.

The vicar . . . well, you never know what you're going to get if you aren't a Sunday regular, do you? This guy, who'd only met Stephen and Jean a couple of times, referred to them – and us, the usual collection of close acquaintances, distant relatives, waifs and strays – as 'dear friends'. At least he didn't add 'in Christ'. And then he summarised Stephen and Jean's lives up to this point as if it were some biblical fucking parable. Lost sheep, found sheep, more pleasure in God's bosom at the stray – or in this case two strays – coming safely home, blah blah. Plus some Prodigal Son stuff. And when he'd finished this pompous reimagining of their lives, some people applauded! That's another thing they do in church nowadays. I think it was the young who started it. I kept my hands by my sides. And when it came to the overwhelming question – I can't remember the newspeak version – the one about knowing any just cause or impediment why the twain should not be joined in holy whatsit, speak now or forever hold your peace, I was half-inclined to say, 'Well, I have been to bed with the bride.' But I displayed heroic self-control at that moment.

In fact, I felt that old mixture of gloom and self-pity approaching. What kept it at bay, funnily enough, was Jimmy, who behaved impeccably, lying between my feet in the front pew. Soon after he had first been bitten, Stephen bought Jimmy a scarlet collar with the word CAUTION running round it. Jean had plaited spring wildflowers into his collar for the wedding, so he was much admired and even petted (by those who couldn't read the warning behind the foliage). However, at one moment in the ceremony I heard a quiet and familiar noise, that of a dog scratching. No harm in that, I thought. But when I looked down, I saw that Jimmy was, very deliberately, removing the flowers from his collar. As if to say, do not offend the dignity of a dog by prettifying him in this way. I smiled as I noted the growing accumulation of petals and stalks on the church floor. And though, like most novelists, I am often tempted by the interpretation or metaphorical elaboration of the everyday, I never for a moment wondered if this incident, when written up, might appear a bit more sinister, a kind of premonition, perhaps; as if to say, all will not be sunshine and spring flowers in years to come. Though if I had thought of that, I might equally have dismissed it as a crappy little bit of symbolism, not one for my book.

The order of service pamphlet they gave out at the church proved a shock. I'm used to them at funerals – and at my age you go to far more funerals than you do weddings – with photos of the deceased at various ages from cheeky little tot to adoring grandparent surrounded by the fruit of his or her loins, and his or her children's loins. I find this all quite touching. But I don't remember seeing it at weddings before. There were six photos, of Jean and Stephen at twenty, Jean and Stephen at sixty – and there, in one of each age, was me – which, given the mood I was in, I found creepy.

And this was compounded by the bridegroom's speech in a flapping marquee, which recounted how I had introduced the pair of them at university, and they had been an item, but were both too young to commit, and so the years passed, and this happened and that happened, and then Julian, the best man in more respects than one, had brought them together again, like a magician, like a *deus ex machina* at the end of a play – except that this particular play had more years to run, happy golden years to come, for which the lucky couple would be eternally grateful to me. And I was thinking, that isn't quite right, that's a bit skewed, a bit *fictional*, when I realised everyone was looking at me, so I did some gesture – shrugging, smiling, palms opening – intended to convey that I was, of course, in a state beyond delight, but didn't want to take any responsibility for my actions, and that it was all down to them now, and if they screwed it up it wouldn't be my fault in any way. Yes, I know there aren't gestures to convey that precisely, but I did my best.

However, that wasn't the end of it. Some of the guests started singing 'For he's a jolly good fellow' which is not something that happens to me often, if ever, and the whole congregation joined in, and Stephen started conducting them, and I looked across at Jean, who of course had a smile on her face, but I knew that particular smile – the sort where you would never be able to guess what was behind it. So I leaned down and stroked Jimmy, who has the main and considerable virtue of always expressing himself clearly, and never being devious. And then, as the reception proceeded to the milling, then the eating, then the dancing, people would come up to tell me that was a wonderful thing I had done, and some had half a tear in their eye, and a few of the women kissed me, and one said she'd call me in as Mr Matchmaker if she needed any help. But I didn't feel like a magician or a *deus ex machina* or even a Mr Matchmaker, and that was when I started to smile and nod vaguely and decided to get drunk. No, not drunk, *very* drunk.

And that's not all, either. You know that bit where the bride tosses her bouquet in the air and whoever catches it gets married next? Well, Jean didn't do that. When someone suggested it was bouquet-throwing time, she walked around the room until she found me flopped in a chair, certainly not in a fit state to drive a car, and dropped the bouquet into my lap. Then bent down and kissed me on the cheek. Whereupon some of the men started up another fitful chorus of 'For he's a jolly good fellow', but I sat back and closed my eyes and so it didn't last long. I was thinking several things. One was that I had only been widowed for three years, and certainly wasn't eager to meet someone new. Maybe Jean was telling me to hurry up – *tempus fugit* and all that. Or maybe she was just feeling sorry and loving towards me. Or maybe it had nothing to do with my condition, and everything to do with hers. Because it was – no, not a hostile gesture, that wouldn't be right. Nor would passive-aggressive. But as if she were saying: I laughed when you made all those funny gestures abdicating responsibility for what happens. But actually, this is bloody serious, this is my – our – last shot at happiness, and yes of course it's up to Stephen and me, but also it isn't. We're all more than grown up – except no one ever really is in my view, we're all just infants in adult clothing (this was often one of Jean's themes), but we're as grown up as we're ever likely to be, and so I'd just like to remind you, Jules baby, that this one is also on *you*, very particularly, and very especially on *you*.

It's possible that she wasn't thinking this at all, or even some of it; but it was what I thought she was thinking that counted.

I looked at the bouquet of spring flowers in my lap, picked it up, bent down towards Jimmy, who was still faithfully between my feet, and began tucking it into his collar. But it was a bit too thick to go through, and I was a bit cack-handed from the wine, so Jimmy turned his head, growled, and bit me. Which I found very funny, because it was further proof that he was incapable of being devious, hypocritical or falsely cheerful, unlike human beings. So I bent down and patted him, and told him of this truth, and he settled down again between my feet.

Naturally, Stephen and Jean had a honeymoon, driving through France and Italy to places which they had mostly visited before with someone else. That must add complication, I found myself thinking. Did they speak normally to one another of these 'someone elses' as they strolled the Promenade des Anglais and gazed up at the Leaning Tower of Pisa? It ought to have been easy, since those previous companions had turned out to be the losers, and Stephen and Jean the winners. But it doesn't always work, talking straightforwardly about previous lovers (and spouses), trying to give them due weight in your life, while emphasising that of course their main function was to be innocent and heedless precursors of the glorious present. Which might feel a little too easy, mightn't it? Even 'simple' curiosity about a partner's previous lovers can lead to envy. Yes, you have 'won', but in this particular case your innocent 'rival' had spent months or years with this person in the prime of their joint lives – a person you have now acquired when both of you are reaching pensionable age. Every emotional situation can easily switch into reverse, it seems to me. And then, as I imagined them working their way south – Lyon, Nice, the Cinque Terre, Tuscany, and then back north again – I wondered if I weren't feeling something akin to envy, if not jealousy, myself? That would be ironic, wouldn't it? But then, why should the emotional life become more lucid and fathomable just because we grow older? Those further years might just provide new grounds and subjects for fucking us up. I've never believed in the serenity of the old – it has always seemed like a fable designed to make them more admirable and us more complacent.

Mostly, though, I tried to think of Stephen and Jean in an uncomplicated fashion, and be excited at having brought them together again. (And yes, that was a true excitement – it's not something that happens every day, is it? I can't think of any other examples, in life or fiction, of such long-delayed reunions. So I felt proud of my part in their success.) But I was also pleased for my own sake – I'd brought two old friends back into my own life as well as into one another's. And that isn't nothing. I'd reached the age where most of my friends from a generation, or even half a generation, ahead of me were dying off. Not that death adopts an orderly, chronological approach to its killing ways. My wife was only sixty-eight when she died.

I'm writing this at the age of seventy-seven, and it is now my generation's turn to die off. Martin Amis likes (soon it will be 'liked') to say, in a melancholy way, 'The trouble is, you can't make new old friends.' I'm guessing he got the idea from Christopher Hitchens (dead at sixty-two). I remember hearing the phrase a couple of times, but not really understanding what they were complaining of. Yes, it's harder making new friends as you get older – but also more gratifying when you do so. Suddenly there is a whole fresh unfamiliar life in your presence, with an undiscovered past and a future yet to be explored – and in the meantime what a lot there is to talk about. This is the joy of 'new new' friends. Whereas if you *were* able to make 'new old' friends, it would surely be an invitation to complacency and blokeish prejudice – to a sort of corduroy-trousered, pipe-chewed bonding awash with sentimentality.

And yet, and yes, something like this had happened to me – I had, suddenly, made two 'new old' friends, even if not quite in the sense originally intended. Here we were again, the three of us, and it wasn't, as you might imagine, full of wrinkly reminiscing: Ah, do you remember the time we went punting and Stephen lost the pole? Whatever happened to old Muckface, who turned out gay in the end, to nobody's surprise? You knew about Henderson killing himself? And so on. Though we did occasionally refer back to university days, it was more that we were caught up in this new *project*, Stephen and Jean, Part Two.

And for me, their story had an odd, extra edge. I've written about love many times in my novels, and few of my characters have ever been granted a happy ending. They certainly don't experience redemption, that Christian concept I have never observed in the real world, except in a very weakened version much favoured by sportswriters. The best I have offered characters is to leave them looking down a long road ahead, uncertain where it will lead, and allowing the reader to decide what they might find on their future travels. Now I would be in the position of that reader, and those travellers.

One thing I noticed early on was how they didn't talk about the years in between – at least, not in front of me. Was this a conscious decision? Had they tried it on their honeymoon and found it led to awkwardness and silence? Or to jealousy and over-curiosity? Perhaps there had been some agreement, overt or tacit, not to look back on those forty 'missing' years. At times, it seemed to me that they were trying to graft their new life directly on to the stump of that time which had ended four decades ago. Even as a metaphor, this might not flourish.

Early on, I had asked Stephen about his previous marriage. He said, almost automatically, as if it were a form of words he had long prepared, 'I married her to forget Jean. A bad idea. She went back to Australia with the boy. I send money.' That was all. Well, it was his business. I never asked if he'd invited 'the boy' to the wedding, but I think the chances were zero.

Also, what was I doing? And what did I expect? That I could somehow pick up with them and continue as if all those years had never existed? And another thing: when they had departed from my life back then it had provoked anger – 'Oh well, fuck off wherever', as I think I expressed it at the time. And how could I expect them to fill in the missing years with and for me, if they weren't doing it with one another? This was not anything I had experienced before. But then, they weren't really 'new old' friends or 'new new' friends, they were something in between. 'New old new' friends?

It happened like this. We saw a fair amount of one another, but somehow without regaining the same intimacy and camaraderie of the earlier years (though why should I have expected that to happen? We had all three changed in ways we were only half-aware of). Stephen and Jean had decided to live close to each other, but not in the same house. I was only half an hour's drive away. And at times it was as if we were two pairs of friends rather than a threesome. And they began to visit me separately. And tell me things.

Jean said, 'I was looking for something in his house and opened a cupboard underneath the washbasin. And do you know what I found? There was an old wooden wine box filled with all sorts of stuff he'd picked up over the years from hotel bathrooms and washbags on aeroplanes.'

I felt she was asking me to disapprove, so I said, 'Sounds harmless enough to me.' If this was the worst she could find after rootling through an unimportant cupboard . . .

'Yes, but he'd made all these little cardboard compartments within it. And each compartment was crammed with – you know, little plastic shampoo bottles, tiny pieces of soap in their wrappers, small tubes of toothpaste and so on. And half the little plastic bottles of shampoo had sort of collapsed in on themselves, I suppose they'd dried out or something.'

'It sounds . . . tidy at least.'

'And then there was one compartment full of little plastic combs, all still in their cellophane wrappers. And *then* there was a section full of little plastic shoehorns, all different colours, about ten of them. I mean, who in God's name is going to need ten travelling shoehorns in their life, especially as he's got a perfectly good normal-sized one in his bedroom, which he actually uses?'

I smiled. I thought this was a bit of an over-reaction.

'It hardly sounds a capital offence.'

'Plus *which*,' she went on, 'everything was covered in dust. It'd been there for years and years. Like it belonged to Miss Havisham or something.'

'Well, if we treat this as a door suddenly opening into Stephen's subterranean psyche, I can think of worse things you might have discovered.'

'Like what?'

'Like, say, a collection of dildos with dried blood on them.'

'That's a disgusting image. I'd been wondering what you've

been up to these last forty years.' Though she didn't, actually, appear shocked.

'Just my novelist's imagination.'

'Oh, don't be so pompous.'

'So what did you do?'

'Threw them all away, shut the cupboard door and washed my hands.'

'Fair enough.'

'I doubt he'll notice. He's an odd mixture of looking carefully and not noticing. Typical man, you could say.'

'Oh, don't be so pompous.'

We looked at one another, and laughed.

Jean lit a cigarette on arrival, and started right in. 'There's a difference between showing your feelings and expressing your feelings.'

It sounded like a rebuke to something I'd said to her earlier, though I couldn't remember if it was. So I merely replied, 'Is there?'

'Yes, work it out, novelist.'

'For instance?'

'For instance, some people are better at one than the other. They try to show their feelings through their behaviour rather than through words.'

'And is the corollary that there are people who are free with loving words but don't back them up with loving actions?'

'Is that so paradoxical?' she replied. 'Can't you think of people who are free with loving words but don't back them up with loving actions?'

'Yes, and I'd call them hypocrites.'

'Then have another think. Isn't it possible, indeed common,

for people to genuinely mean the words they utter, yet fail to back them up with deeds? Or to offer deeds instead of words, and to be sincere in both regards?'

'For instance?' (Though I had guessed the answer.)

'All right. Stephen. Not the biggest leaker of his emotional secrets, you'd agree.'

'I know what you mean.'

'And a few weeks ago there was a piece in the *Guardian* about romantic gestures.'

'Yes, I remember it. I love those vox pops about love and sex, always read them. What women really want. Freud's question. Answer seems to be flowers, and candlelit dinners, and the rest of the usual stuff, but according to this piece the most romantic gesture a man can make towards a woman—'

'—is for the man to run her a bath.'

'Exactly,' I said. 'I was gobsmacked by that.'

'So, shortly after that piece appeared, Stephen started asking me if I'd like him to run me a bath.'

'That's quite sweet, isn't it?'

'Either sweet or autistic, take your pick.'

'So did you call him on it?'

'Of course not. What kind of a callous bitch do you take me for? I said, Yes please. But it's as if – I don't know – as if he's still got his learner plates on.'

'At least he's trying.'

Jean looked at me as if I were defending some rampant chauvinist, not the man she'd married a year previously.

'Trying. Yes, he can be very trying.'

I made a simple rule for myself at this time. Never pass on what one of them had said to the other. Not even a hint, not even if it would have been tactically useful. I didn't want one of them going back to the other with a 'Julian said you said this about me' – not least because it would stop them telling me stuff. Obviously, I wanted them to tell me the whole story, as far as they could. That's what I've been after all my writing life: the whole story. So I recorded a lot of what they said in my diary. And didn't think at the time that this was 'writing about them'.

Stephen rarely had a drink when he came over to talk about things. Partly out of caution: he would be driving home later. But mainly, I think, because his way to truthful explanation lay through clarity and concentration rather than alcoholic relaxation. Something like that, I guessed.

'You know,' he began, 'I'm finding Jean quite hard to read at the moment. What's going on inside her. What she thinks of me, even.'

'Hmm.'

'It wasn't like this when we first got together again. It was as if we'd totally reconnected to how we were forty years ago. It was thrilling.'

It's odd – well, maybe not so odd – how in such situations you quail before the sort of response you find yourself about to give. Things like, 'Well, falling in love is always easier than long-term love.' Or, 'Just because you're in love it doesn't mean you have to stop working at things.' I admit that such clichés were offering themselves to my tongue, so chose silence instead. And after a while, Stephen went on.

'There was a strange moment last week. Maybe it won't seem strange to you. It was seven o'clock, about an hour before we normally have supper, and I said to her, "Shall I run you a bath?" And she gave me a really odd look, as if to say, "What's come over you?" She said, yes, thanks, and I ran the bath and put a glass of wine by the side of it. But I could tell there was something up, and the atmosphere was a bit strained for the rest of the evening, and then we slept separately that night. It's something we do from time to time. It began – well, it was Jean's idea – as a way of keeping things fresh between us – so we don't become two old people in their pyjamas settling down for the night like a pair of aged zoo animals. But lately we've been doing it if one of us has been annoying the other.'

'Like that night?'

'Yes.'

'And it was fine in the morning?'

'Yes.'

Again, the banality-nudge was guiding me towards 'Well, that's all right then, isn't it?' So instead I asked, 'Why do you think she got the hump?'

'No idea.'

'Presumably it was a normal thing?'

'What was?'

'Running her a bath.'

'Well, no actually.'

'You mean . . .'

'I'd never run her a bath before.'

'So why did you think of doing it that day?'

'I don't know . . . it seemed like a good idea . . .' I let the silence extend. 'Well, if you really want to know, I read somewhere that it was something women liked men doing for them. They were supposed to enjoy it. But Jean clearly bloody didn't.'

'Hmm. Just out of interest, can you remember where you read about this being a good idea?'

'Oh, some newspaper article. And I know what you're thinking – I did it because I read about it in the paper. No, I did it because I wanted to do it.'

'My wife had a good phrase for such situations. She called it "practising spontaneity".'

He didn't smile. 'Yes, well, I never met your wife, but I suppose that's funny.'

'I'm only suggesting that perhaps Jean guessed, or felt, that there was something – oh, I don't know – scripted about what you were doing.'

'Whose side are you on?'

'Stephen, I'm on both your sides.'

'Doesn't feel like it. Feels like you're both against me.'

I let that go, and thought we were finished for the evening. But Stephen wasn't.

'You know, when we got together again, I felt really pleased and proud that she'd never been married before. That I was to be her only husband, ever. But now I'm beginning to think that if she'd had a bad first marriage, she'd appreciate me more now.'

'But that's not a nice thing to wish on her.'

'No, I can see that.'

'On the other hand, there is a theory that marriages are like kitchens.'

'Explain, wise man.'

'Well, the first time you put a kitchen in, there's always something wrong with it. Sink in the wrong place, freezer next to the oven. Not enough drawers, too many shelves, and so on. This is what people say, anyway, I've never done it myself. Then the second time you rectify the mistakes of the first one, and get what you wanted.'

I could see Stephen processing this. Eventually, he said, 'Jean's not a kitchen.'

Which was irrefutable.

*

During one of Jean's visits, I decided not just to sit on my couch and listen, but to ask her one or two things directly.

'I remember when I was young, there were three things parents didn't talk to their children about, Politics, religion and—'

'Sex,' she broke in. 'I thought you'd get there sooner or later.'

'Sorry, I . . .'

'No,' she went on calmly. 'It's absolutely fine. And *it's* absolutely fine, as well, as it happens. That's what's so fucking ironic. Fill my glass, Jules baby.'

She'd already drunk enough, as her sudden endearment (unless it too was ironic) showed. So I filled her glass.

'Back in the day, when we were together as students, Stephen was, how shall I put it, a vigorous but undistinguished lover.'

'That sounds a cruel thing to say.'

'Of course it is, but life is cruel, sex can be cruel, and we'll all be dead in twenty years' time. So I'll tell you the truth, and don't you ever fucking use it, not even deeply disguised in some novel where I appear as Jeanette and Stephen is Stuart.'

'Sure,' I said, being far too interested not to promise.

'Ha!' she replied, as if not believing me. 'Of course, at the time, I didn't think of the word "undistinguished". I didn't know enough back then, but I knew I knew more than Stephen. I'd had a couple of lovers, but Stephen was . . . well, it wasn't just that he was technically a virgin, but he had something virginal about him, his manner, his awkwardness, his way of being surprised. So it was the reverse of what was supposed to be the norm – the man knows more and teaches the girl what's what. And there were times when he seemed . . . not shocked, but somehow a bit wary if I appeared to know or want something he didn't know about. If I am making myself clear.'

'Crystalline.'

'And back then, as you'll remember, it was normal *not* to

talk about stuff. You had to go very gently with, No, not like that, like this, darling, and so on. And if you went too far, if you were too helpful, it was sometimes enough to make a man's cock roll over and die on you.'

I held back from responding, not least because I recognised the syndrome myself.

'And then other men came along who really did know a thing or two, and even if I didn't like them as much as Stephen, they were useful . . . teachers.'

'Naturally,' I said automatically, half-wondering whether the reverse had been true in my case.

'So, of course, when I found myself thinking of Stephen in the intervening years, I remembered him in bed as well as out of it. And back then – at university – any sex, unless it was truly awful, was good sex. Indeed, any sex was almost good sex by definition. Almost, yes, almost. And when we got together again, I felt myself apprehensive for all the usual reasons – not that we were about to become a "usual" couple. Things like the ageing body, and undressing, and a different kind of *pudeur*. Plus the fact that my memories of Stephen as a lover were . . .'

'. . . undistinguished.'

'Yes, quite. But.'

She paused, and I did not find myself about to say, 'Oh let's talks about politics and religion instead, for God's sake.' I waited.

'But,' she went on, now with a half-smile on her face, 'that side of things turned out to be fucking marvellous.'

'To coin a phrase.'

'Or marvellous fucking,' she continued.

I felt strangely envious (would anyone have ever said that about me? Or you, for that matter?). I almost told her to Stop right there, but I was greedy for details.

'And the first time, I thought, Where did that come from? And one afternoon, when we had finished, I actually did say, "Where did that come from?" At which he turned on his side away from me, and I thought I'd offended him, and he was assuming I meant which particular lover, or which Thai brothel, did you learn all that stuff from. And there was a long silence which, uncharacteristically, I did not break. And finally, he said, "If it comes from anywhere, it comes from a lifetime of loving you." Which made me feel terribly, terribly guilty.'

'Why?' I asked. 'It doesn't sound like a big problem to me.'

'That sort of response, from an otherwise intelligent man, plus my response, from an otherwise intelligent woman, is precisely why I need to see a shrink.'

'Sorry, that was a bit crass. I hope he's a good one.'

'Yes, she is.' Oh dear, another mistake. But she ignored it.

'Good sex can be as much of a problem as bad sex,' she went on. 'In certain circumstances.' Like most men, I have, in my life, often been blind-sided and wrong-footed by the inner life of women. But this was a new one for me.

Then she went on. 'But I sometimes catch myself wondering . . . If Stephen had been like that as a lover back then, might it have tipped the balance – might we have married then instead of split, married and have kids and grandkids and have been friends with you for the last forty years? But I shouldn't think like that, should I?'

'No, you absolutely shouldn't,' I said firmly, even as some of the mud in my own past was being stirred up.

Stephen would come over from time to time and we'd play chess. Some people think games and sports are reliable indicators of character, but I've never particularly found that to be the case. My own chess game is, or was, solid but unadventurous – I'm a bit of a patient grinder (which I refuse to believe I am in my wider life). Whereas Stephen's was dashing and risk-based (well, quite). At the level we played, however, neither of these strategies proved superior to the other; so usually we were evenly matched. But on this occasion his mind seemed elsewhere, and he rushed into a disastrous bishop sacrifice. I ground him into resignation, then gave him a large whisky and asked how things were.

'Things?'

'Marriage – you and Jean.'

'Oh, fine, thanks.'

No, I wasn't going to let him get away with that.

'I'm not prying' (words we only use when prying) 'but it must be strange living with someone when you've both grown used to being on your own for so long.'

Instead of answering, he said, 'Actually, she did ask me to come along and see her therapist with her.'

'I didn't know she was in therapy,' I lied.

'Well, yes. I don't really like the idea. I think a couple should be able to work out their relationship for themselves. Assuming they're sensible and rational and not bonkers.'

'Neither of you is bonkers.'

'Thanks for the endorsement.' He paused, and I could see he was wondering whether to take the leap. 'The thing is, Jean thinks I love her too much.'

'Ouch.'

'Quite.'

'And what did you say to that?'

'Oh, something like most women complain about not being loved enough. And she said she wasn't most women.'

'She never has been.'

'Anyone would think I was a stalker or something. Or some mad domineering husband. What's that phrase? Coercive control? I don't do that. I always let her come and go as she wishes. She told me the other day she was going away to a spa hotel by herself to clean out her body and her mind. As if I'd filled it with filth or something. Maybe there's a special item on the price list called a Love Detox. Two hundred quid and we'll wash that man right out of your hair. Colonically, no doubt.'

He took a large slug of whisky and asked for more.

'You're not driving home,' I said.

'Ha! That's coercive control,' he said bitterly, or fake-bitterly.

'I just mean I'll get you an Uber or you can sleep here.'

'Do you want me to go now?'

'Of course not, old friend.'

'But I am right, aren't I, that most women complain about being loved too little, not too much?'

'Stephen, you're a clever guy—'

'Ha!' he interrupted. 'She says I may be clever but I don't have enough emotional intelligence. Makes me feel like I'm Exhibit A in some We Sort Out Your Problems column.'

'Can you . . . I don't know how to put it, but . . . why might she think that, about being loved too much? Did she give examples?'

'To tell the truth, I don't even understand the concept. Either you love or you don't love, isn't that the case? And you can't turn down the dial on your feelings, can you?'

'No, but I suppose you can turn down the dial on the expression of those feelings.'

'What does that mean? Stop telling her that I love her? Stop wanting to make love to her? Stop thinking about presents for her next birthday six months ahead and just buy them the night before? Get her a crappy box of Milk Tray and a bunch of daffodils from a petrol station?' He was on a roll, and I wasn't going to stop him. 'Oh, I know, I get it – stop being nice to her. Tell her she's got the wrong clothes on – mutton dressed as lamb, that sort of thing. Be rude to her in restaurants. Not pick her up from the station when it's raining and she's forgotten her umbrella. Oh, I know – I could start slapping her around, couldn't I, that'd show her that I didn't love her too much.'

'Stop it, Stephen.'

'What was that phrase Sean Connery used about hitting women? "A firm slap with an open palm" – that was OK with Sean, he thought that wasn't really like hitting a woman. Listen, I *despise* men who hit women.'

'So do I. And I know you do.'

But the fire continued to burn. 'And the weird thing is, old Sean Connery thought he was being reasonable, being tactful, being *loving*. A justifiable response to a woman who was being provoking or hysterical, or just plain bloody annoying. "A firm slap with an open palm." That delayed his knighthood by quite a few years, I'm glad to say.'

'Getting back to the point . . .'

'Whose side did you say you were on?'

'Both your sides. Always have been. From the beginning. When I first introduced you.'

'Little did you know what you were doing.'

'I was very young at the time, Stephen.'

'And some of us still are.'

'Meaning?'

'Jean. I say this in all sobriety even though I'm drunk, but I think she's scared of love. I thought so the first time round, and I still believe it's the case the second time round.'

'That's a serious thing to say.'

'Yes, and I'll say it to her face and to her fucking therapist's face.'

'Don't do that, Stephen. It sounds like she needs your help.'

'Yes of course she does. It's like one of those old weepie Country songs – "Dial Down Love, Baby". Not "Love Me Do" but 'Love Me Less". I fucking give up.'

'I'll get you an Uber.'

'Perhaps she'll start sleeping around.'

'Thinking that way lies madness, Stephen.'

'Yes, but I half suspected that the first time round. On one or two occasions.'

I'm sure – almost sure – I didn't blush. I just shouted at him.

'Don't even dream of going there, Stephen, or you'll go mad. Just get in your Uber and go home to bed.'

I kept saying to myself, 'But we're all meant to be grown-ups.' And then into my head would come Jean's contention: 'We're all just children in adults' clothing.' But I decline to believe that, it was just another among all the excuses and false self-congratulation ('At least I don't hit her') they were indulging in. They were also getting fed up with my – what would you call it? – fair-mindedness, refusal to take sides, attempts to be helpful. How long, I wondered, was this going on for – and where would it lead?

'Well,' I said to Jean, fair-mindedness leaking from every pore, 'you're both sound of wind and limb and mind, and of a certain age . . . and you've found each other. And were glad to have done so.'

'Past tense noted,' she replied sarcastically. 'As in, any port in a storm.'

'No, no.' I could see she was unconvinced.

'Yes, yes,' she replied. 'Listen, Stephen is the storm, not the port, surprising as it may seem to you. Hurricane Steve, yes I know that sounds silly. But you can't imagine how oppressive it can be having someone in love with you *all the time*.'

'Sounds pretty good to me.'

'Don't be facetious. This isn't some scenario you've invented.'

The other thing I was beginning to note, with a certain resentment, was how they treated me like some useful sounding board, not as someone – that old-new-old friend – who had had a long emotional life of his own, who might even – who knows? – have some *insight*.

'OK. It's oppressive because . . . because you aren't in love with him all the time.'

'Sort of.'

'Or, because you aren't in love with him full stop?'

'No, I do love Stephen, that's a fact. I just wish he wouldn't *be in love* with me *all the time*. Why can't we just settle down into loving one another? We're not twenty any more.'

'But he still is.'

'Sort of.' She frowned, as if she wasn't sure about telling me the next bit. 'But nowadays I find myself locking the bathroom door so he can't burst in and tell me how gorgeous I look in my shower cap and put a badly arranged jug of flowers by the bath and bring me a glass of white wine.'

'Maybe it'll wear off. Can't he take a hint from a locked door?'

'No, he just whines outside, like a dog.'

'Can't you pretend it's Jimmy outside?'

'Jimmy's got more sense than Stephen. For a dog, he's quite good at taking a hint.'

Not for the first time, I found that everything I might say was inappropriate. Like: So he's in love with you, that's one out of two anyway. Or: Why not give him and it more time? Or: Well, if you wanted tact and hint-taking, you should have married Jimmy. Actually, that's what I did say. Because everything I had said so far, to both of them, had been either disregarded or mocked.

'Maybe you should have married Jimmy.'

'I've heard dafter ideas,' she replied, her mood lightening a little.

'So why not give it more time?'

'Because I can't see him changing. Because I can't say to him, would you kindly love me a little less and it'll all be fine.'

'What's that Sondheim song? "Marry Me a Little"?'

'All too true.'

But underneath, I could see she was still intransigent, adamantine.

'Maybe you could make some gesture back which wouldn't cost you much?'

'Like run him a fucking bath?'

'I had been thinking of that, I must admit. But I see it might be a bit . . . obvious. Plus, out of character.'

'Out of my age group.'

'What does your therapist say? Or is the seal of the confessional upon it?'

'She says she's seen such cases before.'

'And?'

'Some of them work out and some of them don't . . .'

'How much does she charge?'

Jean ignored me and lit a cigarette.

'At least I'm free,' I said lightly.

'You're free because you're fuck-all help.'

(Shall I tell you something? I always enjoyed Jean swearing at me.)

Then she pushed further. 'Love, in reality, Mr Novelist, isn't how you and your breed depict it.'

I decided not to take this personally. Also, to ignore the implication that I didn't have much experience of love myself. 'Certainly not in bad fiction. But I think the great novelists understand love, and most aspects of human behaviour, better than, say, psychiatrists or scientists or philosophers or priests or lonely-hearts columnists.'

It sounded a bit pompous, I know. But that's because it wasn't just me who was under attack (which I would have laughed off easily), but all the great writers of the past. Who, as her next words implied, fell short of understanding.

'That still doesn't get us very far.'

'Sorry about that.'

Jean swirled her whisky over the ice cubes and said, in a clear indication that our exchange was over: 'It seems that I am the answer to a question I was never asked, and haven't asked myself.'

It was at that point, I think, that I decided to break my promise not to write about Stephen and Jean.

Later, I began thinking about members of 'my breed' who wrote well about love, whether aphoristically or novelistically. 'In love, there is always one who kisses and one who turns the cheek' – I quoted that in my first novel, and it now seemed appropriate to the present case. Then there was the more famous: 'There are people who would never fall in love if they hadn't first heard it talked about.' I think that's historically been fairly true, though in today's media- and social-media-saturated world, there isn't much chance of someone not having heard of love. And so everyone thinks it's their due.

Turgenev wrote brilliantly about love. So did Chekhov. Both tended to portray hapless or hopeless or catastrophic love rather than wedded bliss. I would have thought that Jean (a Russian specialist when I first knew her) could see that many great writers favoured writing about failed rather than successful love, and that she would therefore have approved of them. Edith Wharton, for another. Perhaps she merely meant – as some solipsistic readers do – that *her* personal case, *her* quandary, *her* way of being unsatisfactorily loved, hadn't been properly described in fiction. Well, I could – and would – sort that out for her. Not that she would ever know. I wasn't planning to publish in her lifetime.

Still, I put my professional pique aside, and concentrated on the matter in hand. I did some research into the situation Stephen and Jean found themselves in (what might we call it? Reattachment Dilemma? Here-We-Go-Again Syndrome?). The classic problem in such emotional revisiting, I discovered, is that the parties unconsciously reproduce the same behaviour which had led the initial relationship to founder. The manipulative continued to manipulate, and the over-possessive to over-possess, but without acknowledging it. Usually, they convince themselves that the intervening years have brought greater – or some – maturity, and assume that they will thereby avoid what had torpedoed their relationship the first time around. But the years have not brought greater maturity; worse, the couples fail to realise that they are, like doomed creatures in some ancient play, cursed to repeat their lives without recognising or understanding that they are doing so. This last sentence, I admit, is mine, rather than taken from some psychiatric journal.

But – as Jean would be the first to point out – their case was not like this. Stephen was so determined to get it right this time – having spent decades berating himself and lamenting his earlier insistence that they could settle their joint lives forever at the age of twenty-one – that he got it wrong again, but differently. It was as if he no longer considered, let alone valued, the forty years of life he'd passed between Jean Part One and Jean Part Two; as if nothing of importance had happened in that time. Whereas of course he had accumulated a series of habits and tics, plus traits of solitude (not to mention a previous wife and child); and he imagined that because he had spent the last thirty years or so comparatively unattached, it would be simple to make a seamless transition from Part One to Part Two.

Jean's position was different. Her interim life had been more fulfilling; she had thought of Stephen with no more than an occasional settled fondness until the day he turned up in her life again. To her, non-attachment had seemed like a kind of freedom, not necessarily sought but easily borne; she wasn't sure she needed or wanted anyone serious in her life at this pre-terminal stage. What Stephen viewed as a rounded, dramatic, necessary conclusion to their two lives Jean saw as – what? – no more than a somewhat intriguing possibility. He was determined only on the reignition of love; she wondered if there hadn't been quite enough love in her life already, and if companionship was the most she actually cared for – in which case, was she not already, and happily, her own best companion?

These are, admittedly, more a novelist's assumptions than an accurate digest of all that they told me; and are inevitably coloured by my own experiences and preconceptions of life. Also, by the stupid, insistent yearning within us all that there should be happy endings for those we love, especially when it seems deserved, and despite whether this is feasible or not. In those old, truthful novels, characters would often read other novels (or sometimes, even more harmfully, poetry) which – being romantic, chivalrous, sentimental and untrue – gave them such misleading dreamworlds that they were inevitably disappointed by real life. Nowadays there are many more misleading fictions – print, film, television, social media, even the simplest TV advert (with clean-smelling clothes, an unshitty baby, a healthy lolloping dog, an attractively chaotic but warmly fun family) – that the specific noxious sources are harder to isolate and quantify.

Only some of the above is relevant: Stephen was no more Don Quixote than Jean was Emma Bovary. They had long ago stopped being dreamers, in their own eyes at least. Stephen didn't see an ounce of fantasy in his plan for them; rather, his past was a fixed and unimportant reality in his mind, and their future just a matter of practical implementation.

Of course, there were times when they seemed like a contented couple, when we were a cheerful threesome, when we did ordinary things together, we three friends and a dog. Such times I rarely committed either to my diary or to memory. One evening that I did, we had all been together at Stephen's house, watching television, with Jimmy fast asleep on his bed. He had absolutely no interest in television, never recognising another dog on it, nor even barking at an onscreen postman. I looked at him and my first thought was foolish and metaphorical. Stephen had won over a Jack Russell with patience, bribery, and an indifference to pain, releasing in the dog a natural sense of affection and loyalty; why should he not win over the dog's owner with similar patience and indifference to pain and make this late-flowering love and long-delayed reunion work?

Then my thoughts wandered to what it was like to be Jimmy. Specifically, to what memory must be like for a dog. Does it understand the concept of time in any way? Or is its mental life a series of repetitive presents with no hinterland? Do dogs have a narrative or episodic approach to their lives, or a bit of both? Though why should his memory work in a parallel but inferior way to how ours does, just because he's another mammal? Then I started imagining Jimmy suffering a left posterothalamic haemorrhagic stroke. If you gave him a bowl of rusks with a topping of leftover lamb, might it trigger instantaneous automatic memories of all the dinners he'd previously eaten? And would that make him salivate to drowning point?

'You were miles away,' said Jean when the programme ended and we decided not to watch the news.

'Yes, I was thinking about Jimmy.'

'That's sweet of you,' she replied.

'And whichever way were your thoughts tending?' asked Stephen in a mock-professorial way.

'Well, I was thinking a bit about memory, and consciousness, the old mind-body problem, and so on,' I answered in a similar tone.

'And did it lead you to an overwhelming question which you might examine in some future part of your oeuvre?'

I dropped the donnish tone. 'No, I was just thinking, Jimmy doesn't know about time, or mortality. He probably doesn't even know if he's a young dog or an old dog.'

'Jimmy doesn't know if he's a young dog or an old dog?' Stephen repeated. 'Listen, Jimmy doesn't even know he's a *dog*.'

And we all found this so funny that we giggled and woke

Jimmy up and petted him, reassuring him that his ignorance of metaphysical questions didn't make him any the less lovable. Stephen and I were just about to set one another off again when Jean said, rather sharply,

'Stop laughing at Jimmy.'

'We're not laughing at Jimmy,' I replied. 'We're laughing at the idea of a dog not even knowing he's a dog.'

'That's still laughing at Jimmy,' she replied.

I was going to sum it up like this:

His tragedy is that he can love, but that his love cannot be accepted.

Her tragedy is that she cannot love, but that what she does offer is accepted as love.

Then I remembered again that we live in post-tragic times. And I was falling into the temptation of the literary trope. Like Oscar Wilde's line that all women turn into their mothers, which is their tragedy, and no man does, which is his. Again, misuse of the word 'tragedy' in a perfectly normal piece of social observation (not that it's *true*, of course, but that's another matter).

So I shall rephrase what I wrote less aphoristically. For instance: where it went wrong was that Stephen believed he was still in love with Jean, and probably was, and Jean could neither accept his love nor return it, which showed either integrity or practical wisdom or harshness on her part. Whether or not she could have loved someone else at this point in her life, and be loved in return, and accept such love, is not within the bounds of my knowing or guessing.

On the other hand, they had each separately said to me, 'This will be my last chance of happiness.' Was this something they each actually uttered, or has my memory altered the words so that they match? I can't be sure. Perhaps the words really were the same, but only because they had already agreed in advance on the formulation. Just as, when students, they had come to me separately and explained they had to either 'marry or split'.

I have been keeping back something Jean said to Stephen. She never spoke these words to me, but I very much doubt he misheard them, or misreported them. Here we go: 'Happiness,' Jean said, 'doesn't make me happy.' It is a thought – also, a rebuke to centuries of fiction – which I have been turning over in my mind ever since.

But, whatever the punchline – and most of our lives don't have one – Stephen and Jean now departed from one another for a second time.

I didn't feel, as I had forty years previously, 'Oh well, in that case, fuck off wherever.' Nor did I, as I had before, feel in any way betrayed. On the contrary, I felt guilt, and also a sense of failure. I had brought them together the first time, in the caff, and then again the second time, in the same place, with the same ultimate result. Yes, I know the second time was at Stephen's asking, but part of me felt as if he were a mere facilitator of my grand plan. And I had been so fucking pleased with myself for reuniting them. Yet I wasn't some noble *deus ex machina*, rather a seedy marriage-broker taking an emotional rather than financial cut from the transaction. I thought I was wise, just because I'd written so many books; I thought I knew what made people tick; I even thought of myself as an advice centre. But I had treated Stephen and Jean as if they were characters in one of my novels, believing I could gently direct them towards the ends which I desired. I'd been confusing life with fiction.

I'll tell you the rest another time. Jimmy is at my feet as I write this. He's an old dog now, even if he doesn't know he's either old or a dog. An existential condition which is at times to be envied.

5
GOING NOWHERE

When I was eighteen, I was introduced to a famous poem by Mallarmé called 'Brise Marine'. It begins, '*La chair est triste, hélas! et j'ai lu tous les livres. / Fuir! là-bas fuir! . . .*' (The flesh is sad, alas, and I've read all the books. / To run away! Down there! . . .) It was quite a stretch for an English suburban teenager to access the mind and sensibility of a prematurely middle-aged French Symbolist poet. My flesh didn't seem at all sad to me (or at least, only sad from under- rather than over-consumption), and I certainly hadn't read all the books. As for fleeing, like many I wanted to flee the parental home, but I didn't want to run away 'down there' – to the tropics. I was far too timid for that. I wasn't Gauguin or Jacques Brel (both buried in the same cemetery on Hiva Oa island in the Marquesas). England was where I understood myself and others, so I wanted to run away to an England – out there rather than down there – which was more interesting, more vivid, more bohemian (though perhaps not *too* bohemian). Which I partly did and partly didn't. As for Mallarmé, he never fled as per his poem – though he did visit England several times.

The immediate ancestor of 'Brise Marine' was Baudelaire's 'Parfum Exotique' (published in *Les Fleurs du Mal* in 1857). The inscription in my Penguin Baudelaire dates its purchase to May 1963, my penultimate year in school, and barely a century after the poem was written. The poet is in bed with Jeanne Duval, who in the language of the day would have been characterised as his 'mulatto mistress'. Eyes closed, he breathes in 'the fragrance of your sultry breast', and a whole landscape comes pre-Proustianly into his mind. He dreams of a languid isle where the men are slim and vigorous, while the women eye you with astonishing candour. There are ships at anchor, and the scent of tamarind trees. Not that Baudelaire, any more than Mallarmé, acted upon these conjured desires. Back in 1841 his military stepfather, despairing of the stroppy twenty-year-old, had put him on a boat to Calcutta; but he never got there, refusing to go farther than Mauritius. And after 'Parfum Exotique' Baudelaire never travelled anywhere exotic; though he spent two years in Belgium at the end of his life.

Rimbaud, the third of that great trinity of French poets, did successfully 'run away' to 'down there!' He fled to the Horn of Africa, where he became a trader and gun-runner. But this was not in response to any poetic self-prompting. He had by this stage abandoned literature forever. What's more, when he got 'down there', far from finding it exotic, he reported to his mother: 'Life here is boring and costs too much.'

Flaubert and George Sand agreed on the difference between the doer and the writer. He declared that no drunkard ever wrote a drinking song, nor any soldier a marching song. She wrote to him in 1866: 'Personally, I don't believe in these Don Juans who are also Byrons. Don Juan didn't write poems, and Byron is said to have been a very poor lover.' She had earlier shared with Flaubert her belief that 'Great artists are often invalids.'

It may well be that for poets back then, the yearning was enough – enough to make the poem, that is. The stay-at-home Philip Larkin ('I wouldn't mind seeing China if I could come back the same day') summed up the whole genre in 'Poetry of Departures', whose narrator hears 'fifth-hand' about a chap who chucked up everything and just cleared off. This temporarily excites the poet, who is just as bored with his domestic life as the escapee; and he thrills to the idea of swaggering the 'nut-strewn road', or crouching in the fo'csle 'stubbly with goodness'. But however alluring, the fantasy will not stick: it is 'so artificial / such a deliberate step backwards', its main purpose being that of helping the poet-narrator to stay 'sober and industrious'.

So the poetry of departure rarely leads to the railway station or airport. However, there is a midpoint between Go and Stay, and a suitable case for realist fiction: set off, pause for thought, recrimination and guilt, then creep back home. John Updike, often seen as a delineator of conventional, continuing suburban America, in fact writes incessantly about flight and dreams of leaving. Harry 'Rabbit' Angstrom is his most famous would-be escaper, who at the start of the Rabbit Quartet flees his family home in a panic and a 1955 Ford; he is heading 'down there' in American terms, southwards from Pennsylvania, only to get lost, turn around, and return to his home town (if not to his wife). In his introduction to the omnibus Rabbit of 1995, Updike describes how, three years before the first volume – *Rabbit, Run* – appeared, Jack Kerouac had published *On the Road*. 'Without reading it, I resented its apparent instruction to cut loose; *Rabbit, Run* was meant to be a realistic demonstration of what happens when a young American family man goes on the road – people get hurt.'

Then there is the additional question of where, specifically, those who flee, or dream of fleeing, want to go. In 1838, two decades before Baudelaire's 'Parfum Exotique', Théophile Gautier published his poem 'L'Île Inconnue'; a mere three years later, it became the sixth and final item in Berlioz's song cycle 'Les Nuits d'Été'. A sea-captain-cum-poet invites a 'pretty young maid' aboard his boat, which is fully prepared and about to sail. His oar, he tells her, is made of ivory, his flag of watered silk, his rudder of fine gold. All permissible and poetic exaggerations, but then he soars into the fantastical: 'My ballast is an orange, my sail an angel's wing, my ship's boy a seraph.' He promises to take the girl wherever she wishes: the Baltic, the Pacific, Java, Norway . . . This high romanticism, or travel porn, is cut by the maiden's reply: she wants him to take her to 'the faithful shore / Where love lasts forever'. The poet-mariner, perplexed by this choice of destination, replies with worldly cynicism that such a shore 'is quite unknown / In the realm of love'. Then he repeats his invitation: 'Where would you like to go / The breeze is about to blow.' It sounds to me as if this particular couple won't be going anywhere.

Do poets still dream of the exotic, but never depart, so that the dream of leaving festers into a poem? Perhaps. But in the nineteenth century, most people never left the boundaries of their village, let alone country, and the few who did often made one single trip which lasted them the rest of their lives. Nowadays, exotic travel has become routine, a gap-year endeavour which parents follow on their Google locators. In place of 'Where would you like to go / The breeze is about to blow' we have the whiff of kerosene as you approach the airport (a smell I used to find as exotic as any sea breeze or scent of tamarind trees) and the lure of duty-free. Back then, they wrote the poetry of departure; today, we write the bucket list.

Do I have a bucket list, now that I am more than three-quarters of a century old? Machu Picchu? Angkor Wat? The Antarctic? An African safari? No, I'm not a geographical completist. I've been to Ayers Rock (when it was called that) and the Atacama Desert, to the Taj Mahal and the Grand Canyon. I've set foot on every land mass except the freezing ones. So I'd prefer to loiter again in European towns and cities, watch the sea from the safety of a promenade and snow-topped mountains from a warm distance. And, just as I shall be rereading great novels for probably the last time, I'd like to make farewell trips to see great art: to Madrid for *Las Meninas*, Brussels for Bruegel's *Fall of Icarus*, Rome for Bernini's *Apollo and Daphne*, Ghent for the Van Eyck altarpiece, Palermo for Antonello's *Annunciated Madonna*, and so on. Maybe I'll be standing in front of a picture I love, fall and hit my head, and be blitzed by IAMs of all the paintings I have loved in one tremendous chronological sequence. It would be Stendhal's Syndrome times a thousand – a grand way to expire, if a tiring one.

Last year, a Belgian interviewer, a woman in her thirties, arrived at my house. As I let her in, Jimmy – whom I inherited when Jean died – wandered out into the hall. He is now sixteen, half-deaf and half-blind and almost comically toothless, so that his guard-dog functions are often both delayed and diminished; while his fierce territoriality has turned into mild curiosity. I explain his great age and debility to my visitor, and she makes much of him. We then have an extraordinarily long interview, of which her culminating question is this: 'So, Mr Barnes, you are now seventy-six, and you will never win the Nobel Prize because you are a white man – are you raging against the dying of the light?' I bat away the first part of the question with a reference to Ismail Kadare, and murmur non-committally about the second. We go downstairs, Jimmy wanders out from his bed, perhaps thinking another intruder has arrived. She bends down, pats him, and asks, 'So, is Jimmy raging against the dying of the light?'

It is not a question either of us has been asked before – certainly not by a literary interviewer. I don't think Jimmy rages about much – he is a stoic who sleeps a great deal. Though he does resent some things, like not being allowed to stop every fifteen yards on a walk, or being given a constant diet of dog food, much preferring human leftovers. When he looks despondently down at some porridgey goo in his bowl, I will occasionally shout at him (not in anger, simply in the chance of him hearing me), 'It's dog food, Jimmy – you're a *dog*.' Though we have already established that he doesn't even know he's a dog.

I am not too dissimilar – I am at least trying to be stoical, and I sleep more since cancer and its treatment arrived in my life. And while I still hate and fear death (though recognising the pointlessness of such protests), do I rage against it? I'm not sure I ever did – I think I tried to wail lucidly against it. And self-pity is hardly relevant when you see how suffering strikes down others, and how ill-equipped many are to deal with it.

For instance, I read this morning an interview with the Villarreal and Spain footballer Virginia Torrecilla, who two and a half years ago found herself suffering from headaches and dizziness. The doctors gave her a CT scan and diagnosed a brain tumour, but a benign one – they could take it out and in a few months she would be training again. After the operation, however, they changed their opinion: it was a malignant tumour, and spreading. Her mother came to Madrid to look after her through thirteen months of treatment: thirty rounds of radiotherapy plus fifteen cycles of chemo. Then, one day, they were out in Virginia's car when a white van hit them from behind. Her mother was paralysed from the waist down and will spend the rest of her life in a wheelchair. Though her car was stationary at the time, and there was no rational ground for guilt, Virginia Torrecilla unsurprisingly went into a deep depression. As she explained in the interview: 'I couldn't understand why this was happening when I've never been a bad person.'

Many people feel like this, believing that life is, or should be, fair, despite powerful evidence to the contrary. With a fallback position that perhaps it might yet prove to be so, at some fundamental level beyond our present understanding. This feeling comes, most probably, from a residue (or even a fullness) of religious belief. I find Virginia Torrecilla's plaintiveness and puzzlement – her innocence in the face of the world's nature – very moving. But we have surely lived enough millennia on this planet to have noticed that life is not fair or just, and that bad things often happen to good people, and good things sometimes happen to bad people, and that sudden chaos lurks constantly beneath each placid surface. When, in the plenitude of her existence, my wife was diagnosed with a malignant brain tumour and was dead thirty-seven days later, I raged against the dying of *her* light, but I didn't imagine that some cunningly concealed fairness or justice came into the matter. Insofar as I could be calmed by any mere phrase, it was one that suddenly came to me back then, and which I continue to employ: 'It's just the universe doing its stuff.' Which will be the case when I too am dying – whether from a mutation of my companionable cancer or a different disease, or from a white van running into the back of my car, or a silent, vengeful e-bike punishing me for not wearing my deaf-aids. So I hope there will be little raging – except over Kadare never getting the Nobel Prize: now that *is* a matter of fairness and justice not being properly dispensed by identifiable individuals.

Two adroit observations about ageing:

1) From my wife Pat, who was six years my senior: 'As you get older, you get hardened in your least acceptable characteristics.'

2) From my partner R, who is eighteen years younger than me: 'You're allowed to be old, but you're not allowed to *behave* like an old person.'

The head and the heart are still working, as the body declines. But better that way round.

The concept of IAMs has inserted itself into my occasional thinking. For instance, the other day I was remembering what Jean had told me about Stephen in bed the second time round. Fucking marvellous/marvellous fucking. And it led me to a daunting thought. What if, in the middle of making love, you suddenly had a cascade of sexual memories, from childish self-fondling through to the doings of last week: all the forgotten moments, from thrilled ecstasies to wan humiliations, and so on. How might we react? With (some) men, it might provoke immediate detumescence; with others, it might even act as an aphrodisiac. And women? I'm not sure I can guess; but some of it would, doubtless, be distracting. 'The flesh is sad, alas . . .'

T. S. Eliot wrote that all we know of other people is the memories we have of the times when we are with them; and that while we are not with them, they – the people – change. I've always found this a bit despairing. But it's also true that even our closest friends and lovers harbour memories and emotions and traits of which we are unaware – and of which they may be unaware too. And I don't just mean that each of us has a box filled with collapsed shampoo bottles from distant hotels, all covered in dust. Or even a metaphorical version of the same.

But those other people Eliot refers to don't just change

when beyond our inspection; they also change in our imaginations when we are not with them. After Stephen and Jean separated, I thought of all the damage I might have done. In the first months after their departures I had an intense and recurring vision of Stephen's car being pulled out of a watery gravel pit, with a skeleton at the wheel still held in place by a seat belt and an exploded airbag. He had told me, 'She's all I've ever wanted, and all I'll ever want,' and I had let him down – worse, I had helped him find his dream a second time, and more catastrophically. How could he not resent me? There is an old cliché, Once bitten, twice shy. But the reality, for Stephen, was: Once bitten, twice bitten.

When I was calculating the damage done, and my responsibility for it, I often forgot Stephen's first wife and 'the boy'. What had become of him, growing up fatherless because Stephen had engendered him while trying to forget Jean? And what became of the boy's similarly unnamed mother?

And Jean? I didn't buy into the notion that she was more self-sufficient than Stephen, that she would soon pick up again the life she'd had until a couple of years ago, all brisk country walks with Jimmy chasing squirrels. I foresaw her in a wasteland of depression, plodding through life blank-minded in a haze of pills, with that white, puffy look I had observed in others. I saw her in a ward with locked doors and plastic cutlery, surrounded by versions of herself which not only convinced her she was part of a community of the deranged, but even made her proud of it: yes, this was the true and logical consequence of her life and character. I imagined visiting her, and finding no recognition in her face, not even a memorious quiver when I spoke her name; and later wondering if this was truth or facsimile on her part, and realising that it made no difference now.

But then came a point when I saw that I was imagining

melodramatic ends for the pair of them – fire and brimstone! – because I wanted to aggrandise *myself*. Look what *I* have gone through by putting *them* through it! As if it had been all my doing. What self-importance and vanity. I told myself again: here were two people, intelligent and largely sane (as largely as any of us is) who, as twenty-somethings and then again as sixty-somethings, had taken certain decisions of their own free will, to love or try to love once, and then a second time. And on each occasion they had taken the sane and intelligent decision that their being together was a mistake, that some fundamental imbalance prevented it from working – even though, as they had each separately told me, 'This will be my last chance at happiness.' Who was I to exaggerate my own importance in this process? It wasn't, as they say, the end of the world: couple fail to make one another happy, well, turn the page and look at the sports results.

But this wasn't right either. It *was* the end of *their* world. And if neither of them finished up in the gravel pit or a locked ward, this didn't make the rest of their lives any happier. We kept in touch by email, but neither of them ever suggested meeting. They each lived alone, consumed by a sense of failure. Some love, and then later grieve for what they had and now have lost. Others try to love, and grieve for not having had something – indeed, they specifically grieve for having failed to have had a life which in years to come might lead to total, utter grief. Does that make sense? Stephen took to drink, but, being him, in a controlled way, when by himself in the long empty hours. Jean travelled, went to spa hotels for a few days at a time, and had a couple of affairs (so I guessed). Cancer got her in the end, of course. I say 'of course' because the percentage of the British population who will get cancer is now one in two. It used to be one in three for my generation (which made me think I might escape it), but now the odds have shortened. Sorry to depress you, if you didn't know. It's partly our own fault for living longer. Of course, treatment is always improving, prognoses generally offer us extra years, pain relief is more effective, and so on. But even so, one in two, eh? Jean, after her diagnosis, decided to let nature take its course. As she put it to her consultant, 'I'm only interested in living, not in merely existing.' A sentiment which many feel, but which often weakens as the endgame comes into sight.

I have a friend whose brother died of cancer thirty or forty years ago. He was in extreme pain, his condition incurable. One day he said to my friend, 'If I were a dog, you'd shoot me, wouldn't you?' Which was true. Nowadays, canine end-of-life care has also improved, but even so. We mostly die like dogs; I've always believed this.

And what did I do with and to Stephen and Jean? After they were dead, I wrote about them; I betrayed my promise to each of them and was parasitical upon their lives. Which of us was the least moral? It's not even a contest, is it?

A scrap of conversation comes back to me. Jean said: 'I suppose the first time round, at university, it was me who decided. So in some way I thought it was only fair to let him decide the second time. Which was stupid.'

Then, after a pause, she added, 'And I was deluded. I was like a teenager after sex all over again.'

I said, 'Maybe we're all teenagers when it comes to sex, however old we are.'

She looked at me dismissively. 'Oh, stop saying wise things that aren't true.'

*

When writing about their second go-round, I remember trying to find words for their condition: 'reattachment dilemma' and 'here-we-go-again syndrome' were all I came up with. Recently, I discovered a word for them: those who part, then after some years seek one another out and fall in love again, are called 'rekindlers'. Whereas those who try to relight the fire and fail are called 'non-rekindlers'. Yes, I agree they sound dismal terms.

Those words come from a survey conducted at the end of the last century by Nancy Kalish, a Californian psychiatrist. 'The Lost Love Project', as she called it, began locally, then spread across the world until she had gathered 1,001 stories (as in the Arabian Nights). Thirteen of those participants were from England, though I doubt either Jean or Stephen would have signed up. The initial break-ups among the 1,001 had been caused by various factors – parental disapproval, a premature leap into marriage (or its opposite, terror of commitment), military service overseas, and so on. Sometimes the couple might have kept in distant, formal touch, as at class reunions; often, contact was only in their dreams. But then, with Facebook and social media, it all became much easier to search, and find, and tentatively explore, and nervously suggest a meeting, and . . .

As a novelist, I naturally prefer anecdote to theory, and if some of the accounts sound a bit cheesy, and others bow to that great American narrative form 'a tragedy with a happy ending', many of the stories are both sincere and affecting. Some of those for whom rekindling didn't work reported that their second romances were shorter than the first; but also that the 'grieving period' which ensued was much more painful than the first time around. This makes sense: imagine all those years of forgetting, half-remembering, dreaming, half-wondering, which might help you through an unsatisfactory life, all leading to what appears to be the ideal solution – indeed, a just reward – only to have your great fire of wanting extinguished as if at the click of a cigarette lighter. How to bear that?

But for a majority, the risk taken was rewarded. Seventy-one per cent reported that the rekindled relationship was the strongest emotional experience of their lives; while couples who had been parted the longest had the highest chance of remaining together. Rekindlers are said to be 'assertive' by nature; though many waited for their potential partner to be separated, divorced or widowed before proceeding (straightforward adultery was to them the least appealing option). But when the couple finally got together, despite first-night nerves, potential physical awkwardness, and so on, the sex was 'volcanic', 'the best ever', 'incredible – almost a spiritual awakening', and so on.

Which took me back to Stephen and Jean, and her unembarrassed account of their lovemaking. But when they broke up, I never asked them how they felt, and whether the word 'grief' was appropriate. Neither of them rebuked or blamed me; equally, both stopped confiding in me. We were all of a generation which was not emotionally blurting. We might discuss our hearts in quiet conversation, but preferred, on the whole, to bear disappointment privately. This is my observation, anyway.

One anecdote among many provided by Dr Kalish's rekindlers has always stuck in my memory. This was the case of a man who turned up for a reunion dinner with his lost love wearing the pair of socks she had knitted for him at high school thirty-eight years previously. Is that touching, or weird? Weirdly touching or touchingly weird? Or just perfectly aimed to make you burst into tears? (And no, I can't imagine Jean ever knitting Stephen any socks – indeed, 'ever knitting' full stop.)

*

That poem by Gautier now exists more famously in its sung version than on the page (and does this make the poem extinct, or rather dead and gone to paradise?). I doubt many read him nowadays, except as part of a French literature course. In my first novel, I quoted approvingly his lines about the immortality of art, how nothing – not even the gods – lasts forever, except for Art, which 'alone endures . . . Great poems last longer than bronze'. I no longer believe this beguiling romantic fantasy. Either we shall blow up the planet, and all art with it, or else we shall survive but evolve into something we cannot even imagine – but nothing like what we are now, with our simple longings for God and love and happiness and art. We shall develop into some life form as distant from us as we are from an amoeba.

Gautier (1811–72) was a poet, novelist, critic and travel writer, convivial and idealistic: '*le bon Théo*' to Flaubert and others. When he died, Flaubert, ten years his junior, wrote, 'With him, the last of my intimate friends is gone. The list is closed.' Three years previously, after the deaths of Louis Bouilhet and Sainte-Beuve, he had written: 'The little band is diminishing.' This happens in time to all literary groups: the 'little band' to which I belonged when I came to literary London half a century ago has been thinned over the decades: by the deaths of its older members – also by expatriation, laziness, crankiness and froideur. The rest of us are now beginning to die out. I learned the other day that Martin Amis is refusing further treatment for his throat cancer. He has already endured severe intervention twice – the second time with a 'last chance' operation involving three separate surgical teams. The treatment he is (quite rightly) refusing is proton beam therapy, which failed to save another member of our band, Christopher Hitchens, whose death was witnessed by Martin eleven years ago. In what was clearly a farewell email to me, he wrote: 'My health is parlous, as you know, but morale not too bad.' I applaud his courage, while simultaneously recalling that he once told me how life was 'thin stuff', compared to literature. I didn't – and don't – agree, but maybe this makes dying slightly easier.

Those lines from Gautier's 'L'Île Inconnue' remind me of what Jean once said to Stephen, and he reported to me: 'Happiness doesn't make me happy.' Stephen cited it as an example of her being at times – if not essentially – impossible to understand. And now, belatedly, I try in turn to understand her. Perhaps she meant that 'happiness' in quotes, i.e., what normally passes for happiness in our world – contentment plus good sex plus friends plus a comfortable way of life – didn't make her happy. That she had wanted to live a more dangerous kind of happiness, one at a higher emotional level than Stephen could supply. Or did she mean (not necessarily referring to Stephen at all) that she had lived at such a high level, but it had never produced such happiness for her; that it was too charged, too tense, too likely to crash and burn. Or maybe it was something else, as described in the Gautier poem but with the roles and sexes reversed. Stephen's dream was of being transported to 'the faithful shore' where love lasts forever. But Jean, like the realistic captain of the unrealistic boat, had implicitly replied that such a shore 'is quite unknown / In the realm of love'. And so Stephen and Jean, like the 'pretty young maid' and the sea-captain, were going nowhere.

It may be that we each mean different things when we speak of love and happiness, within a couple, as well as within society. Especially now. When I was growing up in middle-class suburban England, our family knew no one who was illegitimate or divorced or homosexual; all was heteronormative, and no one saw a psychiatrist unless they were truly, deeply mad. (There were a few minor exceptions: a couple of schoolmasters we thought dodgy, plus a great-uncle who had remarried after his first wife was confined to an asylum.) Now, towards the end of my life, more children are born out of wedlock in this country than within it; divorce, homosexuality and seeing a shrink are routine, while gender has become more fluid. All this is as welcome as it is belated, and we may occasionally feel sharp pity for those in previous centuries horribly trapped in the prisons of social, religious and sexual expectation. Though it would be impertinent to imagine that they understood love less well. They certainly spoke and wrote and made songs about it as powerfully as we can; perhaps more so.

Departure habitually leads to arrival. Not always, of course, as with those poetic French dreamers who never left port. But at train stations, bus depots and airports we gaze at departure and arrival boards. We go, we arrive, we set off in return, and reach home again: we live with this momentum. But these trajectories lie within a larger and more contrary version. In our lives, arrival comes first, and departure comes at the end – except a departure without subsequent arrival. A poet friend, one of our 'little band', when dying of cancer, reared up in bed and whispered, 'Goodbye, goodbye . . .' But he knew he wasn't going anywhere. Philip Larkin's last words, to a nurse holding his hand in the middle of the night, were: 'I am going to the inevitable.' When I was sixteen or so, my English master told the class that he had already prepared what he was going to say on his deathbed: just the single word 'Damn!' Perhaps he meant it simply as a curse at the ending of his life; though his pupils, who were cynical about most of the masters, interpreted it as violent regret for the wasted life he was now farewelling. (I never found out how he died; whether he had uttered, or even remembered, his promised curtain-line, or curtain-word.) I myself am not planning any last words, famous or unfamous; but who knows what might stalk into or out of my brain when I realise that my days are over.

The Departure which will be followed by no Arrival may come suddenly, with no time for thought. But if, as seems most likely, it is to be a death under medical supervision, then there will be a new vocabulary to consider. 'We're just making sure he/she is comfortable,' is one formulaic expression. It's hard for the medical profession to find a lexicon which suits all those who are dying: young and old, lucid and demented, religious and agnostic, terrified and stoic, not to mention their despairing (or, who knows, expectant?) survivors. Recently, the vogue word has been 'pathway'. I remember taking a friend with terminal cancer to a hospital appointment. She sat in a chair while a woman doctor in scrubs knelt tenderly in front of her. My friend said in a puzzled tone, 'I don't know what pathway I'm on.' The doctor looked down at her notes and replied gently, 'The palliative pathway.' 'I thought so,' my friend said. And so the news was broken. Such language will have to do. Paths are generally nice places to be on, quiet, contemplative, relaxing conduits across fields and woods and upland pastures, even if some of them end at a cliff-edge. But 'pathway' is now judged inappropriate by some, as it implies that one path fits all. A suggested replacement phrase is 'personalised end-of-life care plans for individuals'. Some of us will prefer 'pathway'.

It's also enjoyable to discover that today's necessary clichés often have classier linguistic precursors. Prosper Mérimée (writer, critic, author of the novella *Carmen*, saviour of large parts of France's patrimony) died in 1870. Four years later, his letters to Jenny Dacquin, a friend and correspondent of forty years, were published. At the end of his life, after suffering from serious respiratory problems, Mérimée had retired to Cannes. From there, in one of his last letters to Dacquin, he wrote:

> I am still sick and now and then I suspect that I am on the great railway line leading to the other side of the grave. At times this thought is very painful, at other times I find in it the solace one experiences on a train: the absence of responsibility in the face of a superior and irresistible force.

Maybe this is the linguistic solution. Scene: a hospital bedside, a few years hence. Enter a familiar face. 'So, how are you doing, old friend/darling/Mr B?' Smiling weakly, JB replies, 'I'm on the railway pathway.' Those who have read this book will get it. Others will retire while shaking their heads: 'Poor old JB, I asked him how he was and he started babbling about railway lines and cliff-edges. I suppose it's that thing when you get very old and start remembering your childhood. When he was little, he used to watch the trains go by at Acton Main Line station . . . Then he became a trainspotter . . . Or maybe he's referring to his first novel, *Metroland*. Ah, the solipsism of writers . . .'

It's said that, as we age, forgotten memories of childhood often return to us. At the same time, our grasp of the middle years decays. This hasn't happened to me yet, but I can imagine how it might develop as senescence takes hold. Our mental space would be occupied by vivid early scenes, then a long blank, and then a plausible nugatory present, as the repetitive days, and the repetitive confusions, cloud by. Our lives, in other words, would be reduced to a story with a large hole in the middle.

Naturally (yes – as in the way of nature) I am beginning to forget things. Or, more exactly, people. Or, more exactly, their names. Why does the brain do this, obliging us to chase a name we have known for years down back-alley routes which are frequently blocked off, resulting in moments of embarrassment and lying apology ('Sorry, didn't have my glasses on')? Forcing us into defensive manoeuvres like inventing mnemonics, which in turn we may forget. And why is the brain so indiscriminate, deleting names of friend and foe alike? Why not allow us to forget stuff we have little use for, and which we shan't resent not being reminded about? Why does the Circus in our skull abandon us – its runner in the field – at key moments? Doubtless because the metaphor is yet again false: the cerebral Circus doesn't have *intention*. And/or, perhaps it doesn't operate as a monolithic corporation, but has many sections which work autonomously, and are suspicious of one another. And/or, it does its best, but is just as fallible as we are: after all, think of the extraordinary amount of work it's done over the decades, processing, sorting and discarding however many trillion of items of input. How could such a mechanism not have glitches? When I asked my consultant why my bone marrow had suddenly started massively over-producing, thus endangering the existence of its own life-support system (again, a false assumption of *intention* – but a normal one, as how can we not seek for purpose in what happens?), he replied, 'It's just the body wearing out.' And you can hardly blame it, given that humanity's increasing longevity is now forcing it to work overtime – and for no extra pay.

It's just the universe doing its stuff; but even so, it can be exasperating. A few hours ago, for instance, talking to someone on the phone, I blanked on the title of my most recent novel. Why that one, supposedly the freshest in my mind? Why did the brain not let me down over an earlier work – or, much preferably, the title of someone else's book? Why should it do that to me? And for what purpose, except petty humiliation, so that I found myself dumbly referring instead to 'my last novel'.

The only (minuscule) upside to such forgetting that I have so far discovered is this: from time to time I come across a byline on the books pages, or a face at a party, and whereas in the past I might have breathed a silent oath because the bastard had given me that patronising review many years ago, I now find I can't remember whether or not it was indeed him (it's always a him, by the way) and to my surprise feel suddenly relaxed, indeed carefree. No point re-hating him if you can't even be sure it was him you hated in the first place. This isn't much of an upside, I admit, given that it's predicated on a larger downside, but even so . . .

We all know that memory is identity; take away memory and what do we have? Merely some kind of animal existence in the moment. It would be a lesser life form than Jimmy Jack Russell (as I once registered him at the local vet's), who, while now tottery and halting, can still sniff out and recognise his familiar human accomplices, still remember the route of walks and the urine-soaked street corners he prefers to pause at. And he is still able to express pleasure at – or disappointment with – the contents of his dog-bowl.

Every so often, I will look at him and remember my exchange with Stephen. Back then, it had seemed funny that

Jimmy not only didn't know what sort of dog he was, he didn't even know he was a dog. But after a while, it stopped being funny – no, it was still funny, but it started to be sad as well. Not even to know that you're a dog. At least we know that we're human beings. Or do we? It seems to me that humans are often so busy living that they forget they are human – or at least forget what it is to be human, and what its consequences are – and therefore what it means to be dead.

The other day I fell downstairs. It was an interesting experience. I was in the bath one early evening when the doorbell rang. I climbed out, wrapped myself in a towel, and quickly wiped my sudsy feet on the bathmat. When I reached the top of the twelve-step pitch-pine staircase I grasped the wooden sphere of the newel post and said to myself firmly, 'Don't fall down the stairs.' And the next moment my standing foot slipped and I was on my way. I had time in the descent for two observations. First, an awareness that I was picking up speed with the bump of each step; and second, the certainty that I was going to break a bone, or more. As it turned out, I was lucky – I had gone down on my side, which minimised the damage to technicolour bruises lasting several weeks. Had I descended on my face or my back, it would have been much worse.

Not long afterwards, Jimmy fell down the same flight. It was also early evening, and the lights were not yet on. From my study, I heard him go down with the sound of a soft, turning bundle. By the time I got to the top of the stairs, he had already landed on the hall carpet and was shaking himself a few times, as he would if he'd been caught in the rain; then he ambled off to check his bowl for food. At the time it seemed the fall of an episodicist – well, now that's over, so on to the next thing. But his narrativism, or memory, kicked in and he now regards the staircase with suspicion. Sometimes he will crouch on the top step, peering myopically downwards, reluctant to make any move, then anxiously descend with a rocking pause on each step before committing himself to the next; more often, fear freezes him, and he waits to be picked up and transported manually.

This is hardly surprising: Jimmy is sixteen, the equivalent, I am told, of 112 in human years; so he is well ahead of me in decrepitude. He is arthritic, with bowed front legs, and his games-playing, ball-catching, squirrel-hunting days are over; all he chases nowadays is his moulded-fibre dog-bowl, which, in search of the last vestiges of nutrition, he will lick blindly across half the kitchen floor. His feet hurt, and he prefers grass to an asphalt path. He has long sleeps, and is admirably continent for an old animal. Until recently, he used to enjoy humping his giraffe-patterned padded log (though the pleasure of it must have been obscure and symbolic, since Jean had him neutered at a young age); now he firmly ignores this auto-erotic device. He has slowly been going deaf for years, and no longer responds to the dog-whistle, or the human voice; only a loud, firm clap will get through to him. And even so, he isn't able to work out where the noise has come from. He stands and looks in different directions, hoping to spot something reminiscent of an owner. (Can dogs be fitted with deaf-aids, I wonder? Perhaps in America, where death is denied and pets are baroquely pampered.) The one upside to near-deafness is that Jimmy is no longer terrified of fireworks – he used to hide inside the washing machine or underneath the sink on festive nights. His eyesight is also fading faster than mine. He doesn't yet bump into furniture, but seems unable to recognise shapes unless they move: a pair of hands being waved at dog-height is what he waits for. Jimmy and I are more alike in having only about eight original teeth. Some of his were so decayed that they fell out as soon as the vet tried to clean them; now he has a sole canine leaning outwards at forty-five degrees, and the aggressive nips of his maturity have declined into mere gummy graspings. My own mouth is better supplied, but only thanks to a long history of crowns and bridges and implants.

Jimmy used to remember how the front door opened and where the crack of light would appear. Then, for some reason, he started waiting at the hinge side of the door, which made him look strangely stupid. I got him some pills designed to promote blood flow in the brain and ground them up into his breakfast. After a week or so he resumed waiting beneath the latch, as if he had always done so.

I found this rather spooky. And it made me remember an elderly Irish writer I once knew, whose younger wife had put a note on the inside of their front door. Not to point out where the hinges were, but rather to ask, 'T – have you got your key?' We shall all come to it, I thought at the time. I would have been in my forties then, and he eighty-ish. Over supper one evening, T was mentioning another writer of his acquaintance – at which he paused, and asked, 'Is he alive or dead?' Confident in my own memory, I found this a scary indicator of future senility – not to know who was alive and who was dead. Nowadays, I find myself in the same position of doubt from time to time, but it rarely upsets me, because the difference between being dead and being alive seems less marked than it once did. After all, we the living are in an extreme minority compared to those who are dead, plus those who are yet to be born. Which makes life feel like the flimsy moment it is.

Oh, and I checked: they do make deaf-aids for dogs, but

they don't seem to be very successful. I suppose it's hard to do even a basic audiogram. How do you teach a dog to put its paw on a button when it hears a faint *doyng* or *whee* over the sound of rushing water? Old dogs, in defiance of the cliché, can learn new tricks; but not this one, I think.

The first writer I ever knew was Dodie Smith – keeper of many dogs – who in the 1930s had been a highly popular dramatist, and later turned to writing fiction with equal success. She was fifty years older than me, but we were immediately and straightforwardly drawn to one another; later, she appointed me her literary executor. After her husband died, she lived on for a few years in the reed-thatched Essex cottage which she had bought when the money from her plays flowed. Her brain had always been acute and she was 'still Dodie' into her nineties. I used to visit her with her agent, Lawrence Fitch, who as an office boy at the London Play Company more than half a century earlier had been the first person to read and recommend her play *Autumn Crocus*. And it was in his presence that one of the most poignant moments of my life occurred: poignant in itself, but also in what it proposed. Dodie was complaining about her increasing forgetfulness, which spurred Lawrence into gently asking her: 'Now, Dodie, you do remember that you used to be a famous playwright?' And Dodie replied carefully, 'Yes, I *think* so.' At the time, I found this merely very sad; later, I saw the prophetic irony. Here I was, scrabbling about at the start of a literary career. Imagine – just imagine – that you did what always seemed barely imaginable and 'became a writer', even perhaps a successful one, what might nonetheless await you near the end of your life? The forgetting of what you had most wanted to achieve; the wiping from your own brain of all that you had intended and constructed and put out there in the world. Imagine further, say, being blind and bed-ridden when some kind nurse or carer decides you might like to hear the audiobook of one of your novels. They put the headphones on, and you listen to an actor – or perhaps, even, *yourself* – reading words you had written decades previously. And then what? Does it feel half-familiar? Do you think this must be some book you had read in earlier years? Or might it trigger a genuine memory of writing the words? The latter wouldn't be implausible: most of the words I've written are still 'somewhere up there', a fact confirmed when I hear a sentence or two from a book of mine and am often able to feel, if not necessarily quote, the next line or two. So might this be a comforting moment, or a tormenting one?

Why bother with such questions when you can do nothing about them? The decline of your body and brain will continue regardless, and you will be presented with an answer (or not) at the appropriate (or inappropriate) moment. I am well aware of this, but still want to observe things for as long as possible, to the point where I recognise that I can no longer rely on my observations being correct, the point where I shall be bidding farewell to my own self. That would – or will – be a moment, won't it? You might want to savour your departure for a while. Yet it would be swiftly obliterated.

You may find this grossly solipsistic. But I'm not claiming any primacy of imagined pain. I shall be in the same boat as the composer who fails to recognise their own music, the architect who unknowingly admires their own bridge, the golfer who forgets that winning putt, the teacher who gazes unaware at an old school photo, the mother who fails to recognise her own child, the man or woman whose personality suddenly revolts against what it has always seemed to have been, and so on, and so on. When I was in my late fifties, I published a collection of stories about ageing, dissolution and the approach to death. On book tour, I had finished a reading and it was time for audience questions. A white-haired lady raised her hand and said she didn't have a question but rather an observation: 'It's not as bad as all that, you know.' I enjoyed my ticking-off, but still prefer to plan for the worst. And so am a supporter of the charity Dignity in Dying. The Church and the Law have enforced indignity for far too long.

All writers want their words to have an effect. Novelists want to entertain, to reveal truth, to move, to provoke reverie. And beyond? Do they want their readers to *act* as a result of their words? It depends. Occasionally, a young couple will come up to me after a public event and tell me that when they met they were each reading the same book of mine, with the implication – no, the stated certainty – that I had brought them together, by writing the omen of their mutual suitability. Then they beam cheerfuly at me, so I beam cheerfully back, saying, 'Of course, I take no responsibility . . .' and we all laugh. Then there are couples who tell me that on their wedding day they would like to have (or already have had) a reading from the half-chapter about love in my *History of the World in 10½ Chapters*. At which I might make a joke about copyright, or give them a secular blessing of some kind. And while I don't exactly feel responsible, I do feel a sudden apprehension on their behalf, a longing for it to go right, and an alarm that it might go wrong. I feel both emotional and strangely responsible (which is why I deny responsibility). If it went wrong, would they blame me? Probably not, if Stephen and Jean are any guide. So I end up offering somewhat nervous congratulations.

I once wrote a novel about retrospective sexual jealousy, and a husband's fatal obsession with his wife's past. Nearly forty years later, a friend told me of a friend of his who had gone down with a similar psychological ailment. I listened to him laying out the case, and commented, 'Sounds like *Before She Met Me* – maybe he should read that' (i.e., to warn him of the dangers of uncontrolled jealousy). 'Yes,' my friend replied, 'I mentioned it, and he said he'd read it and was using it as a template for what to do.' *Using it as a template for what to do* . . . This made me feel much more nervous than with the wedding couples. Would anyone reading my novel conclude that, as in the book, the rational (or irrational, or at least somehow inevitable) response to retrospective sexual jealousy was self-murder?

Do books have such effects? Goethe's *The Sorrows of Young Werther* is supposed to be the classic example. When Goethe was a twenty-three-year-old clerk in Wetzlar, a friend of his called Jerusalem fell hopelessly in love with a married woman, and despairingly shot himself. Just as Werther was to do, thus putting an end to his Sorrows. The novel was a sensation not just in Germany but across Europe. It had a benign public influence in that it set off a fashion for the 'Werther costume' – a blue tailcoat, brass buttons, yellow waistcoat, yellow leather trousers and high-top boots. Goethe wore it himself, and when he visited Weimar he found that everyone at court was wearing it too.

But the 'Werther effect' was more that just sartorial. It also provoked alarm among some readers at its possible effect. Gotthold Lessing, twenty years Goethe's senior (and 'beyond all dispute, the first critic in Europe', according to Macaulay), feared that it might rush impressionable young lovers into suicide, and others agreed. The book was banned in Leipzig and Copenhagen, while in Milan a priest bought up all available copies for fear of its malign effect on his parishioners. Goethe later described the phenomenon in his autobiography: 'But whereas I felt relieved and enlightened by having transformed reality into poetry, my friends were confounded by believing that they had to transform poetry into reality, imitate a novel like this in real life and, if necessary, shoot themselves.' Does this sound a little too wry and knowing, even self-congratulatory?

And so the legend of a wave of copycat suicides was established. (Though should we not, in establishing cause and effect, also consider poor Jerusalem's 'responsibility'? After all, he started it, and Goethe was merely the conduit by fictionalising his violent deed.) But when Goethe scholars started seeking forensic evidence for the legend, it hardly backed up Goethe's own jocular words – perhaps that's why he allowed them to be jocular. There was the case of Christel von Lassberg, who on 16 January 1778 drowned herself with a copy of *Werther* in her handbag. And Madame de Staël stated that the book had caused several suicides among the most beautiful women of the world, but without giving names and places. Later, in the nineteenth century, male deaths were reported: there are two cases of young men killing themselves 'because of Werther', one by jumping off a tall building with a copy of the book in his pocket; while the other had underlined several passages in his copy of the novel. The lack of further detail is frustrating: why should the early cases be of women killing themselves (were eighteenth-century men less sensitive and more egotistical?). And we also know little of the victims' temperament and previous circumstances. It is easy to want to believe in a great novel's powerful Europe-wide effect; but perhaps the safest conclusion about *Werther* is that of a Swedish public health official, who once declared: 'One case is no case, two is one too many, and three cases is an epidemic.'

I said just now that 'we all know' that 'memory is identity', and that without memory we are just a nothingness adrift. Dodie Smith 'thinking' she remembered being a famous writer, but not convinced. My aged mother 'furious' with me for standing her up three times in a row on the tennis court, when in reality she was bound to a hospital wheelchair. My grandmother in old age believing that her daughter (my mother) was in fact her youngest sister, who had died of TB sixty or more years previously. Three women at different stages of 'losing it', it being their own identity. No memory, no identity.

Yet now I am not so sure. Those of sounder mind and memory note what the demented are losing, what their brains are misplacing, what they're getting wrong. At the far end of the scale, we say (or used to say) that he/she's a vegetable, as if all animal as well as human life had leached away. In 1870 Jules de Goncourt, demented by tertiary syphilis, died. His brother Edmond chronicled his decline: forgetting the titles of all his books, then the arrival of 'the haggard mask of imbecility'. At one point Edmond asked Jules where he was. 'Away in space,' he replied, 'in empty space.' 'He' was still 'there', even if the words didn't mean what they previously had. Jules and his mind were in a place they had never been to before. Yet he was not dead, he still answered to his name, he was still 'himself' underneath 'it all' – at least, that's what his brother thought, as we do when faced by a demented person we love. They haven't turned into someone else. Even that pillar of the community, who has lived a straight and straitened life, and now suddenly bursts into senile coprolalia, has not been taken over by another person, another spirit (much as we might like to believe it). His coprolalia was probably always up there in his brain – as it might be in all our brains – waiting for some trigger, as with an IAM, to sluice it out. So we might be tempted to conclude that while, for practical purposes, memory is identity, and identity memory, in absolute terms some identity, however unhinged, however unmoored, seems to survive. However much it dwells 'in space, in empty space', however unrecognisable it may be, it is still there, even when memory is gone.

On the other hand, this could just be sentimental hopefulness on our part, a refusal to admit that total absence is perfectly possible before the final absence. Nor shall we be able to report on the truth of the matter when we are far down that path – or pathway.

We all have different attitudes to ageing and its terminus, from blank denial to insistent, life-smothering over-attentiveness. My mother, in her seventies and eighties, would refer to 'an old boy in the village', or some 'poor old thing' who'd had to go to hospital, as if she herself didn't qualify for the word 'old'. At most, she might be 'getting on a bit'.

I have a friend who, when her husband started showing frailty in his seventies, remarked: 'It's not what I signed up for.' But any such non-signing would have been mute and internal. Promising *not* to look after your wife or husband isn't an option in the Christian wedding vows, or their secular equivalents. In sickness and in health, for richer for poorer – no, stop, scrub that, I'll just agree to the health bit and the richer bit. That wouldn't go down very well with the congregation.

My wife kept a small notebook in a bathroom drawer. I asked her what it was. 'It's my Diary of Decrepitude,' she replied. Given that to me she appeared in full radiance, I didn't take it seriously, and certainly wasn't interested in looking at the evidence. Now that notebook is on my desk, and I have just opened it for the first time. It starts in March 1995 (when she was fifty-five) and its final entry is in September 2007, a year before she died. The first entry is 'physio for tendonitis in right hand'; then pain in left arm, weakness in right wrist, '?tennis elbow', laser treatment on left cheek for scar, physio for left shoulder. Then there are the pills and creams she took – Pro-Gest, Retinova, DHEA, Fibrogel, Efudix, St John's Wort, minocin, lacrilube, solaraze, feldene gel, and (unnamed) sleeping pills. She notes pains in arms, legs, and shoulders; ear-hoovering, a burst blood vessel in her left eye, rib pain, styes, treatment for Morton's neuroma; sudden flushing, rosacea, shivers, nausea, skin rashes, swollen joints, possible arthritis and emergency laser treatment at Moorfields for a retinal tear. These may sound like the jottings of a hypochondriac, but she was never such, and rarely mentioned any of these treatments to me, or would brush them off with a joke. I would call them instead the anxieties of a perfectionist. She was also a stoic, bold and largely fearless, one who approached death, when it suddenly appeared, with a brave equanimity. The last page of this tiny notebook has been torn out, but on the endpaper there are the faint inky negative images of what she had written. I did what any character in a novel – usually a thriller – would do: went into the bathroom and held a bright light on the page while looking at it in the mirror. But this isn't a novel, let alone a thriller, and I couldn't make out a single word.

We take illness so personally, don't we? What else can we do, given that it's happening to *us*? Yet there is also something grossly impersonal about it.

Do you remember when the theft of catalytic converters was rife? A couple of pseudo garage mechanics would arrive in a van, quickly jack a car up, and in ninety seconds the converter, containing all those rare metals or whatever, would be ripped out and the men would be off. An old friend and neighbour of mine, disturbed by a noise from the street, opened his bedroom curtains and saw a man half-underneath his car. He rushed down to the front door and shouted, 'What are you up to?' The man stood up and pointed at him. 'This has *nothing to do with you*,' he said in a threatening manner. 'Now *fuck off* back inside.' Which my friend obediently – and wisely – did.

I sometimes think of this incident when I'm musing on illness and decrepitude. It's just the universe doing its stuff, it has nothing to do with you, so just *fuck off* back inside, OK? Do you see what I mean?

There is memory, and then there is death, which erases all memory. Leaving survivors with memories of the dead, which seem at first as vivid and full of motion as when the person was alive. But this is a brief illusion. In January 1943 the fighter pilot and memoirist Richard Hillary was killed on a night training mission; he was twenty-three. Three months later, Arthur Koestler published a memorial tribute in *Horizon* magazine:

> Writing about a dead friend is writing against time, a chase after a receding image; catch him, hold him, before he becomes petrified into a myth. For the dead are arrogant; it is as hard to be at ease with them as it is with someone who has served with you in the ranks after he received his commission. Their perverse silence has a numbing effect: you have lost the race before it started, you will never get hold of him

> as he was. Already, the fatal legend-forming mechanism is at work: those pleasant trifles are freezing into Biographical Anecdotes, and weightless episodes hang like stalactites in the caves of your memory.

I am writing this an hour or two after hearing of the death of a great friend, the publisher and fiery spirit Carmen Callil, whom I have known for forty years. No, tenses change with death, and I should write 'whom I had known' (but I resist this). I saw her three days before she died – she had stopped her cancer treatment and was at home in bed – and we chatted and laughed and held hands for nearly an hour before I told her that I'd always loved her and we kissed goodbye. Knowing as I arrived that this would be the last time I would see her, I had reminded myself that a dying Carmen Callil was still more Carmen Callil than she was dying. As indeed she proved: the next day a mutual friend went to say goodbye, and Carmen characteristically reported to her: 'Jules came and told me he had always loved me – though not in a fuckable way, of course.'

I agree with much of what Koestler says, especially about petrification and Biographical Anecdotes. Carmen was a great fund of stories, told by her and about her, which will keep her alive, while also – by their repetition and the unlikelihood of their being added to – confirming her deadness. But I can't agree that the dead are 'arrogant', that they are like newly created officers, let alone that their silence is 'perverse'. This seems far too harsh: as if, having suffered extinction, the dead are now to be morally judged. And how can their silence be 'perverse' when speech is not an option?

I don't think Carmen – though she was a Dame of the British Empire and a member of the MCC – will ever become officer-class in my mind and memory. She was far too subversive and effervescent. 'Bursting with life' is a cliché, but one not quite dead, and applicable here. It was as if life – more life than a body was capable of holding – was inside her and just came spurting forth. I remember a group of us waiting for her in the upstairs room of a restaurant; we heard her rising footsteps, and then, while still invisible, she announced, 'Carmen's here!' as if to say, Now the fun can begin. And I think she will burst into my future memory like that too; and take longer to petrify than anyone else who might die while I am still alive.

There may be a few more Biographical Anecdotes yet to come, which will characterise her and last. But I think the adjectives her friends use to describe her will pale first. Just now I called her 'fiery', to which I would add: warm, funny, fierce, clever, loving, angry, bustling, tireless, committed, curious, quarrelsome, pleasure-loving, sociable . . . and as I write them they seem wan, deathly wan. I think an Instagram clip of her singing 'Now Is the Hour' with her great friend and fellow-publisher Liz Calder at a birthday dinner of mine will depetrify her more than any of these adjectives. And she will never become officer-class in my memory because in life she was republican, anti-establishment, anti-patriarchal . . . oh dear, more moribund adjectives. Find better ones, then, you may rightly demand. But maybe the adjectives we usefully apply to the living lose their lustre when applied to the dead.

Also, I may well be wrong about the Biographical Anecdotes drying up after someone's death. For instance, the other week, I went back to my old school for a fundraising event. Among the audience was a man, shortly to turn eighty, who decades previously had sat at the next desk to my brother in class. He told me that his parents had been friends with ours (something of which neither my brother nor I were aware);

and that one day, his mother had returned from visiting our mother and reported of her: 'She looked like she was standing over a drain.' The anecdote delighted me, the more so as it remains ambiguous. Was our mother being unwelcoming, was she suddenly pitying her lot, suffering from dyspepsia, or an attack of *Weltschmertz*? And at this distance – thirty-six years after her death, perhaps seventy after the original event – we shall never find out.

Henry James, ever wise and subtle, put it like this. In 1892, remembering his late friend James Russell Lowell, he wrote that one of death's effects is that it 'smoothes the folds' of the person one had known. 'The figure contained by the memory is compressed and intensified; accidents have dropped away from it and shades have ceased to count; it stands, sharply, for a few estimated and cherished things, rather than nebulously, for a swarm of possibilities.'

When I was younger, one of my rules was 'write each book as if it will be your last'. It wasn't my sharp awareness of death which impelled this self-instruction; rather, a quiet pressure to ensure that I made the work as good as I was able. This was a necessary pretence – like writing as if my family were dead even though they weren't (and not that I wanted them to be). I doubt either rule made any of my books better or worse than they might have been. But in more recent years, writing each book as if it could be my last has had a harsher, and also more practical, edge to it. And from time to time I've had the subthought, 'This wouldn't be a bad one to go out on.'

Ten or more years ago, I gave two long-time friends and

students (or rather, professors) of my work, Vanessa Guignery and Ryan Roberts, what we billed as 'The Last Interview'. I felt I had been quizzed to death over the previous thirty years, and it was time to make an official vow of silence. But within six months, with a new book out, I found myself back giving interviews, talking about the book – yet again – until the point where my actual memory and grasp of it became skewed. Recently, the two of them have proposed what we might call 'The Second Last Interview' or 'Definitely the Last Interview'. If so, we'll see how long I keep that vow.

There is also a sense, or a vivid fear, that after forty-four years of being published, I must be beginning to repeat myself, coming back to the same old tropes and memes, rehearsing my favourite quotations from my favourite authors, even (though I hope not) repeating my jokes. Occasionally I consult Ryan and Vanessa as to whether I've used something before. For instance, a few years ago I asked them if I had ever written a scene in which a young man (not unlike me) arrives with his parents (not unlike mine) at the house of his parents' friends for dinner; the son has a pair of mirror sunglasses peeping out of his top pocket. The host, a short and irascible Belgian mining engineer, without a word of greeting, rips them out and waves them around with the words, 'These are a piece of shit!' I felt I must have used this scene, or a version of it, because it had been such a vividly remembered incident from my own early life. I had acquired the sunglasses in Hungary in 1965, during a six-week van tour with friends behind the Iron Curtain, and was absurdly proud of them – even if they had a suggestion less of Hollywood star than of Communist secret policeman. Our host's aggressive reaction was for me a moment of fierce humiliation, increased when my parents pointedly declined to react (perhaps they agreed with their friend). It had left such a burn that I felt sure I must have used it somewhere, somehow. But after consultation, Ryan and Vanessa concurred that I had never previously deployed this incident. So then I did.

This is a simple form of repetition, against which there are known defences (like looking the story up in digitised editions of your books – though I prefer to use the memory of friends). Yet as for the wider stuff? I can hardly ask Ryan and Vanessa if I have written about death before, or love, or France, or memory. And while I may feel I still have something more to say on these matters, what might seem fresh to me may appear stale to others, even the most sympathetic. My wife used to say that she wouldn't retire until they came up with a different verb for it; or until someone pushed her back against a wall and said firmly, 'You can't *do this* any more.'

There are multiple examples of writers who have gone on and on and on 'doing this' into their old age, typically lapsing into the easy garrulity of autobiography (most writers' lives can and should be summed up, not least by themselves, in a single volume). After my wife died in 2008 I found it natural and necessary to talk aloud to myself as I moved about the house, but every so often I would issue a routinely stern correction: 'Shut up, you're *boring* me.' Not that I bore myself when I write – it is one of the times I feel most alive and original – but therein lies the trap.

There can be another factor. A writer (also critic and academic) whom I knew passingly over many years was the South African Dan Jacobson. He was wry and gentle in manner but fierce in argument. I first met him in the late 1970s as a fellow-contributor to the *New Review*, then lost sight of him for decades. (Another narrative with a hole in the middle.) More recently, I used to encounter him while each of us was gently nurturing his decrepit cardiovascular system with a stroll in the local park. I ran into him for the last time near the local farmers' market, to which he had been despatched by his wife. He showed me an empty meat pie tin from Little Jack Horner for which he had been instructed to buy a refill. I asked how he was. Not great, he said, because he had stopped writing. 'Since when?' 'A year.' 'Is it lack of concentration, lack of interest?' I asked. 'No,' he replied, 'disgust.' I didn't understand this at the time – there was nothing about Jacobson's work to suggest that this might be a proper authorial retrospect – but I think I do now.

There are more flamboyant ways to announce an impending silence. V. S. Naipaul, while publicising one of his later novels, declared on radio that the Novel was Dead. Ergo, the listener understood, Naipaul wouldn't be writing any more. And ergo further, and hilariously, no one else should either. When subsequently asked about his diktat, Naipaul denied that he had ever made such a declaration: he couldn't possibly have said it, because he didn't believe it to be the case. What he did believe (and what an idle listener might have misconstrued) was that the novel form came to fullness, and therefore completion, during a period of fifty or sixty years in the second half of the nineteenth century. All fiction written thereafter, he declared, was nothing more than 'a pale imitation' of what had gone before.

But this, in a way, was an even more startling claim, and a different kind of self-immolation, because it provokes the question: when did Naipaul come to this truth about the novel? Was he aware of it as a young man, in which case he was committing himself to a literary tradition he believed to be exhausted? Or did he slowly notice it as he went from novel to novel, gradually understanding that he was dealing in (and providing his readers with) nothing more than pale imitations? In which latter case, what a terrible and crushing realisation this must have been.

Happily, the novel-writing community tends to ignore such decrees, even from one of its more distinguished practitioners, and goes on its merry, various and repetitive way. And the novel-reading public ignores it as well, being less interested, and less noticing, of any theory of decline and imitation, taking its pleasure regardless, sometimes reading contemporary fiction for its portrait of a shared time, but also earlier fiction for different worlds and shared truths. And both communities will continue for many decades to read the best novels of V. S. Naipaul.

As for me, I am now seventy-eight, and this will definitely be my last book – my official departure, my final conversation with you. Finishing my last book in my own time and then going silent at least has this useful consequence: it means that you will not be cut off – as Brian Moore feared – in the middle of writing. In this way, you are denying agency to death. Though in a very minor way, admittedly.

Once a book is published, there develops a certainty around it. Everything looks planned, in its right place, as always intended. Whereas during the book's making, the writer is constantly uncertain – will this connection work, am I being over-explanatory (or over-subtle), should I entirely rethink the structure, and so on. With completion, the book also solidifies in the writer's own mind. You forget all the stumbles, the seductive but irrelevant trails you followed then abandoned; sometimes, you even forget where the idea first came from. Then, with publication, the book is read and interpreted in different ways, some of which you generously allow, others of which you courteously decline. No, this novel is not a homage to *Jules et Jim*; nor that one 'a subtle riposte to Derrida'; nor my latest a '*roman-à-clef* and tribute to an old friend'. But the book will settle itself down (whatever the critical response) and an assumption of clear, unflustered intent will normally seem apparent to the reader.

So – to return to Proust – it now feels to us absolutely right and immutable that in *À la Recherche* the gates of memory are unlocked by the crumbling of a madeleine into a cup of lime-flower tea, just as Proust's Aunt Léonie had done when he was a little boy. The madeleine is a perfect emblem because it is moulded in the shape of a pilgrim's shell, and Marcel is setting out on his own pilgrimage in search of lost time. And yet . . . and yet, in 1907, when Proust was working on the first volume of his novel, it was a piece of stale bread dunked in a cup of tea which had sent him on his exhilarating journey into the past. And in the next version, it was a piece of toast. And sometime in 1908, a kind of hard biscuit. Had he settled on any of these, we would readily have applauded their rightness, noting how rich memories can spring from humble sources, just as – in Proust's own comparison – torn-up pieces of paper, when placed into water, may be transformed into Japanese flowers. How right and proper any of these preparatory notions would have seemed. And had we learned that back in 1906, say, Proust had initially thought of a madeleine, and then scrapped the idea, we might well have agreed with this decision, judging it both too cosily autobiographical, and also too pointed an image: pilgrim's badge – the path of memory like the route to Compostela – no, that's just too *pushy*, too arty, too knowing – what a relief that he chose instead that hard biscuit or that piece of stale bread – quite right to hold back on the over-fanciful – Marcel, you're a true artist!

During the Covid lockdown, after first laying in long novels and bread-making machines, people started getting rid of accumulated clutter from cupboards, attics and cellars. With municipal recycling centres closed, items were left on pavements and steps and front walls to be taken away. And miraculously, there was always someone who wanted something, whether a plastic implement of mysterious purpose or a collection of old VHS tapes. And the habit has continued, at least in the part of London where I live. The other day I was going through a pile of discarded books when I came across a paperback published in 1967 by the Consumers Association called *What to Do When Someone Dies*. I didn't take it for myself – I think I have learnt the emotional and bureaucratic protocols of death by now – but for a friend with elderly parents. It is a bit out of date, in the main financially. Back then, the minimum cost of a funeral, including burial or cremation fees, came in at £75; while a stillborn child could have a funeral or cremation from 'about £5 to £7'.

What struck me most, however, was the handbook's opening sentence: 'You may discover someone apparently dead, and it can be difficult to tell whether he is really dead or not.' And then, a few sentences later: 'If there is any doubt whether someone is dead, treat him as being alive.' I find this very comforting advice. But then (my imagination reaching for the worst option, as it habitually does), what if you found yourself comatose in a gutter, unable to call for help, with indifferent strangers looking away in disgust, and relying on the hope that one of them might have read the sixth sentence of *What to Do When Someone Dies*?

*

Jimmy Jack Russell died a few months ago. And this week Ismail Kadare followed him – still without winning the Nobel Prize.

So, in conclusion, I am going – literally – nowhere (and you are too, I'm afraid, my friend, but stick around as long as you can, if only for my sake). I am aware that shortly I shall exist as only a shelf-ful of books plus a cluster of Biographical Anecdotes. And life is not a tragedy with a happy ending, despite what religion promises; rather, it is a farce with a tragic ending, or, at best, a light comedy with a sad ending. Or, in the old formulation, it is 'a comedy to those who think, and a tragedy to those who feel'. The first person I loved, contemplating her future death, once said to me, 'I shall miss finding out what happens.' I hope the future won't be as bad for you as it currently looks – but then, perhaps it only appears chronically bleak to me as a tactic by my subconscious to minimise the dismay of my dying. Fifteen years ago, when I was writing a book about death, I was still beset by night terrors, being hurtled into consciousness in the middle of the night with a vivid sense of eternal non-existence and a cry of alarm – sometimes I would have precipitated myself out of the bedroom and on to the landing before realising where I was and how absolute my non-future was. Though I still think about death every day, such vivid actualisation is now in remission. 'So, Mr Barnes, are you raging against the dying of the light?' No, not so much. I feel a little more accepting of it, a little more philosophical.

Is this because I have finally attained some maturity? 'Ripeness is all', as Edgar puts it in *King Lear*, a play I first read at school over sixty years ago, when the concept of 'ripeness' seemed implausible, as I looked around at the world. My parents and grandparents and their friends didn't seem 'ripe' in any way, they merely seemed *old* – some middle-aged old, others old-old; none of them ripe, at best only wizened. 'Men must endure / Their going hence, even as their coming hither', Edgar urges in the immediately preceding lines. Not that, on the whole, we 'endured' our coming hither, for all the screaming we might have done at the time. (A thought: what if we could, with a well-placed pinprick in the brain, provoke an IAM of our passage down the birth canal and into a nurse's latexed hands? I'm aware of rebirthing therapy, but have always doubted whether its results were real. Not that those being rebirthed are faking it, but it seems more an act of the imagination than a true recuperation of memory. If the experience came as an IAM, we might deem it more truthful. Though for myself, I'm not sure I would like to revisit my mother again in such circumstances. I'd rather revisit her when she was making sandwiches on a sunny afternoon.)

I don't think it's the arrival of ripeness that makes me philosophical; rather its opposite, an acknowledgement of decay. Parts of my body have been slowly malfunctioning for decades. ('No sooner do we come into this world,' said Flaubert – and yes, Ryan and Vanessa, I know I've quoted this before, doubtless more than once – 'than bits of us start dropping off.') Glasses in my late twenties; Ménière's disease in my late forties, with partial loss of hearing and deaf-aids soon to follow; a decade later a virus removed most of my sense of smell (though fortunately not of taste); then blood cancer in my early seventies. This last assailing has an interesting side effect. As I said, myeloproliferative neoplasm is not going to kill me unless it mutates. But neither can I kill it: chemotherapy is merely defensive, keeping the disease's berserkness at bay. So my cancer and I will trundle along arm in arm until the day I die. At which point, yes, there will be a 'victory' – I, in dying, shall have killed my cancer! Barnes 1, Cancer 0 – result! Though as I write this (and my mind again reaching for the grimmer scenario), I realise that the presence of one cancer does not rule out the future irruption of another. I have a friend who is currently hosting four of the bastards. So the result could be a thumping defeat rather than a meaningless victory.

And I think I'm glad I'll be dead before full access to the brain's workings is achieved (though I wouldn't mind *trying* a cascade of IAMs). If humankind cannot bear very much reality, I suspect it also cannot bear too much knowledge about itself. We can only live successfully – or 'happily' – it seems, by consciously or unconsciously limiting our knowledge and our reality. Too much of either might drive us mad. We understand this, and with a tactful horror close doors upon ourselves.

Obviously, as an agnostic/atheist, I don't see many upsides to being dead. Only minor consolations are available. The luck of my lifetime (largely peaceful, with many greater freedoms than for previous generations), and the luck of my life (free from poverty, unmaimed by religion, largely happy, always interesting – at least to me – and in its second half professionally successful). And there is another, negative kind of consolation, much grimmer, in what I might escape: the world burning while those in power indolently look the other way; the high chance of a nuclear winter, whether brought about by accident or malevolence; the potential destruction of democracy, still the least worst form of government we have found; and the relentless defeat of altruism by self-interest. The future looks apocalyptic, although this might be the delusion of one awaiting, if not already on board, Mérimée's lulling train to the cliff-edge. Hmm: 'cliff-edge', no, that's too melodramatic an image for death. The train's terminus will merely be what Georges Brassens called *la fosse commune du temps* – time's communal grave, its anonymous boneyard.

I shall 'miss' 'you' – whatever that means. Each word in that phrase is weakened and undermined by death: that 'shall' becomes – or will become – meaningless. And now, at the last, I have no grand pronouncements to offer, no famous last words. (Though I came across a good example recently: the first Lord Grimthorpe's urgent, dying message to his wife, 'We are low on marmalade.') Instead, let me thank you for your sturdy presence – invisible yet lurking, like my cancer. When asked how I see our relationship, I reply that I am not a didactic writer. I do not tell you what to think or how to live. I do not write *ex cathedra*: novelists shouldn't speak down to readers from an assumption of greater wisdom. Instead, I prefer an image of writer and reader on a cafe pavement in some unidentified town in some unidentified country. Warm weather and a cool drink in front of us. Side by side, we look out at the many and varied expressions of life that pass in front of us. We watch and muse. From time to time I will murmur things like: 'What do you make of that couple – married, or having an affair?' 'Look at those fashion victims, so pleased at being themselves it's almost touching.' 'Where's that priest off to in such a hurry?' 'What does that kiss *mean*?' 'An old couple holding hands – that always gets to me.' 'Do you think he's a tramp or an artist?' 'Is that a quarrel, or just a lovers' playful riff – it's a bit Chekhovian.' 'Look, a Jack Russell, now there's a lucky omen.' 'There can't be rain in the air, can there?' 'Do you think there's a God – you know I don't.' 'And why are they looking at *us* all of a sudden?' Ordinary, conversational mutterings, one (or none) of which might possibly metastasise into a story. Out of the corner of my eye, I see that you share my attendingness.

But I rarely catch your replies – you're sitting on my deaf side, I'm afraid.

Still, I hope you've enjoyed our relationship over the years. I certainly have. Your presence has delighted me – indeed, I would be nothing without you. So, I'll just rest my hand briefly on your forearm – no, don't stop looking – and then slip away. No, don't stop looking.

Julian Barnes
London, 2022–25

ACKNOWLEDGEMENTS

I should like to thank: Jean-Pierre Aoustin, Ray Dolan, Dr Claudia Fugazza, Vanessa Guignery, Hermione Lee, Michelle Montague, Sumaya Partner, Ryan Roberts, James Russell and Galen Strawson.

A NOTE ABOUT THE AUTHOR

JULIAN BARNES is the author of twenty-six previous books, for which he has received the Man Booker Prize, the Somerset Maugham Award, the E. M. Forster Award from the American Academy of Arts and Letters and the Prix Médicis and Prix Femina in France. In 2017 he was awarded the Légion d'honneur. His work has been translated into more than forty languages. He lives in London.